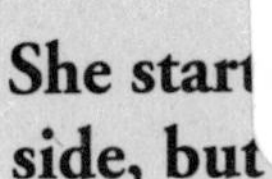

She start

side, but

her face in his hands.

“Don’t do that,” he said. “All those snowflakes caught in your curls make you look like a princess.”

She lifted her chin, and the tiny droplets of melting snow on her face seemed to glisten. “How can this frog be a princess when she’s never been kissed?”

That was all Isaac needed to hear.

He sucked in a breath, not giving his mind time to think or to worry or to even care about tomorrow.

“I can take care of that right now,” he whispered.

He closed his eyes and slowly guided her face to his, relying on sense, rather than sight, to that first taste he knew he would never forget.

And Autumn did not disappoint. Her lips were soft and warm and surprisingly insistent upon his, and in the haze of their kisses he felt her fingers on his chest, unbuttoning his coat.

Books by Harmony Evans

Harlequin Kimani Romance

Lesson in Romance
Stealing Kisses
Loving Laney
When Morning Comes

HARMONY EVANS

loves writing sexy, emotional, contemporary love stories. She is a single mom to a beautiful daughter who makes her grateful for life daily. Her hobbies include cooking, baking, knitting, reading and, of course, napping. She works full-time writing and managing digital content, and has over fifteen years of experience in internet marketing.

Harmony received the 2013 Romance Slam Jam Emma Award for Debut Author of the Year. In addition, she was a 2012 RT Reviewers' Choice Awards double finalist (First Series Romance and Kimani Romance). She is a member of Romance Writers of America.

Connect with Harmony at www.harmonyevans.com for the latest news on upcoming releases.

WHEN MORNING COMES

HARMONY EVANS

HARLEQUIN® KIMANI™ ROMANCE

This book is dedicated to my daughter,
who has made me richer than I ever thought
I could be with her enduring love.

ISBN-13: 978-0-373-86363-1

WHEN MORNING COMES

For questions and comments about the quality of this book please contact us at CustomerService@Harlequin.com.

HARLEQUIN®
www.Harlequin.com

Printed in U.S.A.

Dear Reader,

I just love a hot man in a business suit, don't you?

Isaac Mason is an ambitious, intelligent and sexy investment banker. But is he also committing fraud, or is he simply the victim of blackmail? That's what Autumn Hilliard, a private investigator, has been hired to find out. As she gets closer to Isaac, Autumn discovers that he is hiding more than just the key to his heart. And it's got nothing to do with cold, hard cash.

When Morning Comes is my fourth novel for the Harlequin Kimani Romance line, and I hope you enjoy it. I love to hear from readers. Contact me 24/7 at www.harmonyevans.com.

Be blessed,

Harmony

Chapter 1

"I will not tolerate anyone destroying what I've worked so hard to build. Paxton Investment Securities must prevail unscathed. Is that clear, Ms. Hilliard?"

Sterling Paxton, the firm's owner and CEO, stood at the boardroom window with his back to Autumn, his pale white hands clasped loosely behind him. His stance was relaxed, yet every terse word sounded as if it were uttered through gritted teeth.

A chill threaded through Autumn's spine, warning her to keep her guard up even as she sat frozen in place.

So this was what a bug must feel like, she thought, right before it's about to get squashed.

Sterling turned abruptly on his heel and smacked his hands together.

"I said, is that clear, Ms. Hilliard?"

Autumn winced and drew in a sharp breath before smiling sweetly. "Of course, Mr. Paxton. I'll do everything in my power to prevent that from happening. If Isaac Mason is committing securities fraud, rest assured, I will find out."

Sterling's lips thinned. "How long do you think that will take?"

Autumn resisted the urge to shrug, knowing he would be offended. Every client expected immediate results and it was her job to manage expectations. She was a damn good investigator, but she wasn't a miracle worker.

"A few weeks. Maybe a month. Undercover work is never an exact science," she cautioned.

Sterling slid his hands into his pockets, and she heard the tinny jingle of coins.

"Isaac must never know he's under surveillance."

"And he won't," Autumn affirmed with a nod. "Having Isaac mentor me as a new employee will enable me to build trust without arising suspicion."

Sterling's gaze narrowed. "For your sake, he better not."

Autumn bristled at his veiled threat, but she said nothing. It was obvious Sterling didn't trust Isaac. What she didn't know was why, but she'd surely find out, on her own terms and in her own way.

"You have full access to all his files, reports and records," Sterling continued. "I sent you the log-in information to our internal file system via email last night."

He crossed the room and sat at the head of the table.

The leather chair squeaked under the weight of his large frame.

"You and I are the only ones with knowledge of why I hired you," he said, folding his hands slowly. "Not even my daughter, whom you'll be meeting shortly, knows about this."

Autumn sensed extreme urgency in his tone. "I understand the need for confidentiality," she reassured him. "As soon as I have something of interest, I'll report back."

The conference room door opened and a tall, slender blonde entered into the room with a thick sheaf of papers in her hand. She closed the door behind her and glared at Sterling. But when she saw he wasn't alone, she took a step back and Autumn watched as her face quickly morphed into a smile that was as fake as the handbags sold on a New York City street corner.

The woman moved toward her and extended her hand. "I'm Felicia Paxton, director of human resources. You must be Autumn Hilliard."

Autumn stood. "It's a pleasure to meet you."

She shook Felicia's clammy hand and silently wished for a tissue. She was five feet eight, and Felicia towered over her in an oppressive way that was probably intimidating to a lot of people. But not to Autumn. She wasn't afraid of anything, except failing to solve a case.

"Please have a seat," Felicia instructed. She turned to Sterling and glanced at her watch. "It's 8:55 a.m. now. The meeting was supposed to start at 9:00 a.m., correct?"

"Yes," Sterling answered in a bored tone, not bothering to look up. He seemed engrossed in scrolling through his smartphone. "We were just chatting while we were waiting for you."

A blush washed over Felicia's taut cheekbones. She walked around the table, pulled out a chair and settled down directly across from Autumn.

"In addition to being CEO, my father seems to love to do my job."

Autumn took Felicia's contentious tone as a subtle warning that anyone who dared trifle with her had just better think twice.

Sterling eyed the stack of papers Felicia had on the table. "Not that part," he barked. "With the level of technology that's available today, why is it that our employees still have to fill out all these forms?"

Felicia uncapped a pen and held it out to Autumn. "Two words, Father. Paper trail."

Autumn produced one from her notepad, not from her ear, where it normally hid in a mass of natural curls.

She held it up. "I have one, thanks."

Felicia frowned, as if she took it personally that Autumn had her own ink. "The government still loves killing trees," she continued. "And I for one have to agree with them. Paper is more permanent. Electronic records can be hacked or deleted."

Sterling's eyes narrowed and caught Autumn's. "My daughter seems to have forgotten that paper can be shredded," he said dryly.

Felicia ignored him, but Autumn could almost feel how much she wanted to roll her baby blues at her father.

With one finger, she pushed the stack of papers toward Autumn. "I prefer you complete these now, but if you must, you can bring them back tomorrow. I'm here by 7:00 a.m. sharp every day."

Autumn nodded and dutifully began to fill out the ream of paperwork, starting with her social security number. It was as fake as the new identity the government had bestowed upon her a few years ago. Just one of the so-called perks of settling out of court in one of the most high profile cases of corporate fraud in the United States.

She was just starting to fill out her name when the door suddenly opened. Her head snapped up, curls brushing against the side of her jaw, as Isaac Mason walked into the room, his stride purposeful.

It only took one look and Autumn knew this was one man she wouldn't mind sticking close to all night long.

Isaac wore a tailored gray suit cut to perfection, a crisp white shirt, maroon silk tie and black leather shoes shined to a gloss. It was standard corporate attire and likely designer, based upon his wealth and prominent position in the company, but she couldn't tell and didn't care. It wasn't his clothes that attracted her.

It was his face. Isaac was boyishly handsome with clean-shaven, mocha skin, a long straight nose that flared out just enough to be interesting, and full lips that invited lust.

Autumn found it especially difficult not to openly stare at his lean, muscular body. There was something irreverent about the way it seemed almost caged beneath the fabric of his suit.

So as discreetly as possible, she sized him up. From the top of his close-cropped black hair to the tips of his Brooks Brothers shoes. Because that's what private investigators were supposed to do. No one could blame her for trying to do her job even in the midst of extreme male temptation.

And in her professional opinion, one fact was clear: Isaac Mason was her hottest suspect yet.

Isaac shut the door and held up his smartphone. "Sterling, sorry I'm late. I just got your meeting request."

He stopped midstride, his eyes zeroing in on hers. From a distance, she couldn't see what color they were, but they mesmerized her just the same. Luckily, she was able to maintain a mildly curious look on her face, although on the inside she felt her professional resolve begin to disintegrate.

"Am I interrupting something?"

Only the normal rhythm of my heartbeat, Autumn thought.

"Not at all." Sterling waved him over. "I have someone I'd like you to meet. This is Autumn Hilliard, our newest analyst on the Paxton team."

Autumn swiveled in her chair and stuck out her hand. Before she could stand up, Isaac's skin warmed her palm and his smile instantly carved its way into her heart. It seemed that he held her hand a beat longer than necessary, but that could have only been her imagination. She was pretty but not gorgeous, and Autumn had a feeling that Isaac was used to the latter in his ladies.

He gave a little bow. "Welcome to the madness."

Isaac's voice had just enough depth to rumble in her ears, his tone pleasant and slightly mocking. He seemed distracted by something, and she wasn't vain enough to think it was her.

Sterling openly scowled. "Isaac, I realize the market is slightly down this morning, but you're going to be spending a lot of time with Autumn, so let's keep things positive, okay?"

Autumn's face tingled. The negative vibe in the room was getting more uncomfortable by the moment.

Isaac slipped his phone into his pants pocket. "You know me, Sterling." He shrugged calmly. "I was just playing."

He dropped into a chair next to Autumn and leaned back. She smiled and held his gaze, a tactic she used to build rapport with a client, a potential suspect or a man who was really, really cute.

An unbidden spark pulsed between them, like the feeling one gets when suddenly remembering a long-forgotten dream, and Autumn knew that she'd have to be careful not to succumb to temptation.

Suddenly Isaac shot up in his chair. "What do you mean we're going to be spending a lot time together?" It was as if he'd just now grasped the full extent of what his boss had said moments earlier.

Felicia's eyes narrowed at Autumn and Isaac before turning her attention to Sterling. "Yes, Father. Explain."

"That's why I called the meeting," Sterling bellowed, ignoring Felicia's glare. "For the next few weeks, Isaac, you're going to be Autumn's mentor. Getting her acclimated to the way we do things around here."

Out of the corner of her eye, Autumn saw Felicia's hands tense.

"M-mentoring!" Felicia sputtered. "What are you talking about, Daddy? My new employee onboarding process doesn't begin until next month."

Sterling pressed his index finger on the table and shook his head. "It starts now, Felicia."

"But the process hasn't been fully vetted," she protested.

Sterling shrugged and leaned back in his chair, as if the matter was settled. "What better use case than a real scenario?"

Felicia smoothed her blond-in-a-bottle hair. She was probably very pretty when she smiled, but that wasn't the case now.

"Legal won't like it," she warned.

He gave a disgusted sigh. "Have you forgotten that our in-house attorneys report to me?"

Felicia threw up her hands in exasperation. "I haven't even completed all the required documentation."

Sterling looked up from his cell phone and rolled his eyes. "Great, just what we need. More paperwork."

Autumn cast a glance at Felicia and stifled a laugh. If she had a pencil, paper and an artistic bone in her body, she would sketch two plumes of steam erupting from each of her ears and fire blazing in her eyes. The woman looked that angry.

Sterling's phone beeped loudly and he stood. "You'll have to excuse me. I'm due at another meeting in a few minutes." He handed Isaac a manila folder. "I'll leave you two alone to get acquainted."

Autumn smiled at Felicia and she could almost see the wheels turning in her head. Her gaze lingered on Isaac for a moment, as if that would lure him away. She seemed to sense something that neither Autumn nor Isaac could have imagined.

Sterling opened the door and exhaled impatiently. "Felicia, are you coming?"

Autumn tapped the stack of papers with her pen, breaking the tense moment.

"I'll have these back to you this afternoon."

Felicia rewarded her with a nod and a thin-lipped smile.

"Right behind you, Father."

She waited until Sterling was gone, and then rose from her chair slowly, as if she were still reluctant to leave.

Autumn felt Isaac's gaze upon her cheek. She dug the toes of her shoes into the carpet in a vain attempt to hold on to the twinge of pleasure that zoomed through her body.

"Isaac," Felicia said sharply. "Be sure to show her my office, won't you?" Her voice suddenly dropped to almost a whisper, like dark silk hiding a double-edged sword. "You know the way."

Without saying another word, Felicia quickly walked out of the room, closing the door behind her, leaving an empty vacuum of silence and longing.

The statement was an invitation for Isaac, backed up by veiled warning meant for any woman who might interfere.

Namely, Autumn.

But what Felicia didn't know was that Autumn wasn't a threat to whatever hold—real or imagined—she had on Isaac. Sterling hadn't hired her to bed the man, although at first glance the thought did cross her mind. No, she was here to conduct an investigation into a possible case of corporate securities fraud.

Autumn didn't know what, if anything, was going on between the two of them, but if it affected the outcome of this case, she would damn sure find out.

Chapter 2

Isaac leaned back in his chair and almost smiled at the irony. He hadn't been expecting a beautiful woman on the agenda for Monday morning. Then again, he'd never expected to be cooking breakfast every day for two children, either.

Or trying to cook. His kids were not pleased with having to settle for Pop-Tarts. Again.

He sniffed lightly wondering if the stench of burned bacon was still on him and what Autumn would think if it was.

Isaac mentally slapped himself upside the head. If he cared even a little bit about the opinions of this perfect stranger, this gorgeous stranger, the stress must be really getting to him. He had two children to think about now, not impressing a woman.

He was a father.

"Anything wrong?"

The concern in Autumn's voice sounded so genuine, he nearly blurted out, *Everything.*

And it was true. His life was in a state of total upheaval right now. Sure, the chaos was the result of choices he wanted to make, but that didn't make things any easier.

Instead Isaac opted for the answer likely echoed in countless offices across the country on any given morning. Men and women just like him who wished someone would care, but who also realized that most people were too busy just trying to make it in this crazy world to bother.

He faked a yawn. "I was running late and missed my morning coffee."

Isaac kept his gaze trained on the boardroom window. The mid-January sky was a bleak and dirty gray, the kind that makes you wonder if the sun will ever shine again. For reasons he didn't understand, he didn't want to look too deeply into Autumn's eyes. It wasn't that he was afraid of what he would see in them, but of what he wouldn't.

"I don't drink coffee."

Her voice wove through his ears, piercing the fog of his thoughts. It was throaty, insistent and knotted with just enough innate sexiness to make his groin twitch in a way that made him glad he was sitting down.

Just to be on the safe side, he rolled closer to the table and turned his head toward her.

"What mortal doesn't drink coffee?" he said in an

incredulous tone. "What gets you up in the morning? Your extremely good looks?"

No sooner were the words out of his mouth that he realized he'd overstepped the boundaries between simple curiosity and workplace etiquette. Rule number one: never acknowledge the physical attractiveness of your coworkers.

He hated the fact that his stomach clenched as he waited for her reaction, but Autumn just sat there with a blank expression on her face.

If Felicia was still in the room, she'd probably write him up. Ever since she tried to seduce him and he'd turned her down, he'd been paying for it. She watched him like a hawk circling prey.

Did she really think he was stupid enough to bed Sterling's daughter? His working relationship with his boss was strained enough without any additional help from Felicia's shenanigans. Although Isaac doubted Sterling knew anything about Felicia's unwanted advances, he couldn't be sure without actually asking him.

Still, Isaac had a nagging feeling that the partnership he'd busted his butt working for his entire career was now out of reach, and he didn't know why.

Autumn's voice broke in on his reverie. "No. What gets me up in the morning is," she replied, leaning forward, as if in secret. "Pure. Adrenaline."

Her plump lips, coated with just a hint of pale pink gloss, turned up into a very kissable half smile. She seemed amused rather than offended at his statement, which made her even more attractive.

Her perfume, the scent of a flower he recalled but

at the moment couldn't name, teased his nose. At that moment, he knew he would drive himself crazy trying to remember and wishing he could smell more of her.

Isaac whooshed out a breath of relief. "Ah, yes. I remember those days."

The times he couldn't wait to get to the office. He was always the first to arrive, the last to leave and the chump who didn't mind coming in on weekends and holidays. All B.K.

Before kids.

Thank God, they'd saved him.

Autumn settled back in her chair. "So what happened?"

Isaac's heart squeezed again at the caring in her voice and he drummed his fingers on the table under her intense gaze. Although the question was a legitimate one, he wasn't about to tell her—or anyone else—the truth.

"The world's financial markets collapsed one by one. Making our jobs a whole lot tougher. You need more than adrenaline to survive in this business now. You need a magic wand and the ability to predict the future."

Autumn's warm laugh resonated throughout the room and sank into his bones, and for a moment he felt carefree and relaxed.

Her expression quickly sobered. "That's part of the reason why I'm here."

He frowned, sorry to see her smile disappear but suddenly knowing why. "Another victim of downsizing?"

Autumn nodded. "We'd lost so many clients that it didn't make sense to keep all our analysts around. Or at least that's what they told me."

He couldn't imagine being jobless. In the past, it was something he'd never had to worry about. But with the way Felicia was acting toward him lately, he wasn't so confident. Since she was Sterling's daughter, nobody at Paxton really knew how much influence she had over him. To be ensnared in her web was one place no employee ever wanted to be.

"Their loss is our gain," Isaac replied with what he hoped was a reassuring smile.

Her exuberant grin was infectious. "Thank you. I'm really excited to be here and to be working with you."

Autumn tilted her head and he watched her curls skim the edge of her jawline. He wondered what that hair would feel like in his fingers. Her white, long-sleeved silk blouse did not detract his eyes from coveting what was beneath. In his mind, he saw his hands around her trim waist as she hitched up her navy blue skirt.

Isaac's groin tightened painfully and he shifted slightly in his seat as his body involuntarily reacted to a sudden desire for Autumn that he didn't understand. But he did know this: furtive glances at her across the cafeteria or in a meeting room would never satisfy him.

He bet that, beneath the stark corporate garb, she was as soft and fleeting as the snowflakes that were beginning to swirl outside. Yet he sensed she was tough to catch and even tougher to hold on to. That's why he had to stay as far away from her as he could manage.

He picked up her résumé to distract himself. There was no current home address listed, but he assumed she lived in the area. As was his custom, he flipped to the last page so he could review her work experience in reverse chronological order.

Reading quickly, he learned that Autumn had a bachelor's degree in Economics and Mathematics, and a master's degree in Statistics. All from Yale University. She was an Ivy girl, she was smart and she loved numbers. Plus, she had a killer body. It added up to some serious trouble for a man who was trying not to be attracted to her and failing badly.

"I hope you won't let our respective universities affect our working relationship," she said in a teasing voice.

He glanced up from the paper in front of him. "You're referring to the long-standing rivalry between Yale and Harvard."

She nodded and crossed her legs, sheathed in sheer hose he yearned to rip away.

He smiled. "A little bit of competition always makes things more interesting, no?"

"Most definitely," she responded. "But I'm glad I'm on your team, rather than fighting against it."

Isaac raised a brow. "Because you know you would lose?" he said matter-of-factly, hoping he didn't sound arrogant.

She shook her head. "Not at all. But winning isn't everything."

Isaac glanced over at the door. "Don't let Sterling ever hear you say that."

Autumn didn't ask why and Isaac was glad he didn't have to explain. If she wanted a career at Paxton, she would learn for herself soon enough.

He returned his attention to her résumé and noticed something that puzzled him.

Like Autumn, Isaac had also made the decision to pursue an advanced degree directly after college. But the difference was that when he finished graduate school, he'd gone straight to work for Paxton, which was one of the leading investment firms in the country.

On the contrary, Autumn had worked at some mid-level investment banks all around the country. Los Angeles. Phoenix. Miami. Companies whose names he'd never even heard of.

He considered pressing the issue but decided against it.

Multiple job hops might make some people nervous, but not him. Autumn was young, intelligent, and she obviously knew when a situation wasn't working to her advantage. Ambitiousness was a quality he admired, especially in a woman.

Besides, if Sterling trusted her enough to hire her, why shouldn't he?

Still, he couldn't let her off the hook completely. "Your résumé is impressive," he began slowly. "But you've moved around a lot. Surely that's not because of the economy every time, is it?"

"I always leave myself open to the possibilities of a greater challenge or something new."

He flipped back to the first page again. "Your previous place of employment was in Cleveland?"

Autumn's lips curved into a mischievous grin. "What can I say? I love to rock and roll!"

Isaac laughed aloud, pleased by the free-spirited tone

in her voice. He found her playful attitude refreshing and very appealing. Even in the overbearing atmosphere of the boardroom, not to mention the pressure of the first day in a new job, she had no problem being herself.

Most women tried everything they could to impress him. The girls in the office knew he was single, available and one of the wealthiest men in New York City. Out on the street, the women knew him as a regular guy who was hotter than the asphalt on a July afternoon. In the winter, they worshipped the ground he melted ice on.

He'd be the first to admit that sometimes he took the bodies they willingly offered and he enjoyed them. The one-night stands most of these women hoped would turn into a lifetime of ardor and passion meant absolutely nothing to him.

While the opportunity to bed a beautiful woman and run the other way the next morning was still there, now he had two good reasons to refuse their advances. His children.

Consequently, he hadn't slept with a woman in a very long time. Whether becoming a father caused him to feel a sense a guilt or greater moral virtue, he didn't know.

The more likely reason was that he was tired of being a pawn in a two-player game that never went anywhere. Of pretending he didn't want a woman to love him for more than his face, his body or his money.

Isaac checked the time on his phone and stifled a yawn.

He'd been up late again helping his son, Devon, with

his math homework. He couldn't remember the last time he'd had a good night's sleep. And tonight, he expected that thoughts of what Autumn looked like without the corporate jail suit would impede his rest even further.

"What do you say we rock and roll and get a jump on that tour?"

"Sounds great," Autumn replied. "You can show me the cafeteria and we can finally get that cup of coffee you missed out on this morning."

Isaac tried to swallow back another yawn. When it escaped, they both laughed.

"Yeah, you can tell I really need it, can't you?"

His eyes caught hers again. God, she was even prettier when she laughed. Thank goodness, the analysts occupied a space on another floor in the building.

His phone beeped, bringing his attention back to business. He pulled it out of his pocket, looked at it and groaned.

"Unfortunately, the tour is going to have to be a quick one. I've got another meeting in ten minutes and I think I've used up all my Get to a Meeting Late cards for the day."

"How do I snag one of those?" Autumn joked.

"Trust me, you do not want to be in Late Club," he said, in all seriousness.

"Why not?"

"Because I'm the one and only member." His gut did a little flip when she pursed her lips at him. "I didn't used to be," he backtracked. "I mean, it was only when I—"

He stopped abruptly at the winsome look on her face

and realized he was rambling. Something that was completely out of character for him. Worst of all, he'd almost told her about his kids. No one at Paxton knew about them and he wanted to keep it that way for now.

"Just do your best to never be late to a meeting, especially one with Felicia or Sterling," he said curtly.

"I appreciate the heads-up," Autumn affirmed. "By the way, is there always that much tension between them? My neck was beginning to hurt watching their verbal ping-pong match."

"Yeah," Isaac snorted. "But you'll get used to it. We all have. Felicia plays the Daddy's-girl role around here to the hilt, but she's very capable."

And lately very dangerous.

Isaac had heard rumors of people getting terminated, supposedly because Felicia didn't like them, but those were typically lower-level employees. They were the unfortunate ones she liked to trample on the most.

Hopefully, Felicia knew better than to mess with him. Isaac had too much stake and longevity in the company to throw it all away just because of her passive-aggressive antics.

If only he could figure out why Sterling was giving him the cold shoulder all of a sudden, then he'd be able to come clean about his kids. They meant more to him than anything in the world, and being made a partner at Paxton would secure his new family's financial future.

He wouldn't let anything or anyone stand in his way.

Not a bitch like Felicia.

Nor a beauty like Autumn.

Isaac felt her eyes examining his face, as if it would

reveal all his secrets, so he got up and walked over to the floor-to-ceiling window.

The snarl of people far below seemed to belong to another world. He always liked to remind himself that he was one of them, especially during those times he was afraid of losing everything.

"Can I ask you a question?"

Isaac turned away and faced her. "Sure, anything."

"What do you like best about working here?"

Isaac took a few steps and leaned against an empty console.

"That's easy," he replied. "I get to play with other people's money, and make a bundle of my own. What about you? What attracted to you Paxton Investment Securities?"

She folded her arms. "The reputation of the company in the industry. Plus, the fact that I love to analyze every investment to insure we are maximizing profits and shareholder value while maintaining the highest ethical standards in every transaction."

He was surprised that her bold confidence excited him, making him stir in all the wrong places. When a woman's strong work ethic was a major turn-on, that's a sign that one was severely undersexed.

"You sound like Sterling," he said with hidden admiration. "No wonder he hired you."

Although he truly meant it as a compliment, she brushed his comment aside.

"I just try to do the right thing, in any and all situations."

"That's wonderful. That's the way it should be," he asserted. "You are reporting to Sterling, right?"

Something flashed in her eyes. "Wh-what do you mean?"

He gave her a strange look. "He's your boss. You're his direct report, not mine, right?"

Autumn nodded. "Yes. Sorry, I blanked out for a bit."

Isaac was relieved. At the moment, he worked solo and that's the way he liked it. Having to manage Autumn would be a major distraction, one he couldn't afford to risk right now.

"It's kind of an odd arrangement, isn't it? That analysts report directly to the president of a firm. Especially one of this size."

Isaac shook his head. "Not at Paxton. Sterling wants there to be a clear division between the investment bankers and the analysts. He feels it's easier for the analysts to remain objective and impartial, in order to avoid any conflict of interest.

"Have there ever been any issues?"

Isaac clenched his jaw. While he appreciated her curiosity, she needed to know that there were some questions that were off-limits at Paxton. But it wasn't his place to tell her that. All he was supposed to do was give her a tour of the building and that was it.

Ignoring the question, he eyed the stack of paperwork on the table. "We'd better get a move on it. You'll want to get those forms filled out and turned in quickly. Paxton has one of the best employee benefits package in the industry, especially if you have—" He choked back his secret. "I mean, if you're married or have a significant other."

Not reporting a life change, namely the adoption of his children, was another rung Felicia could hang him by. But if he reported it to her, she'd run to Sterling and tell him right away, and that would be the beginning of the end of his career at Paxton.

Even though Sterling had a daughter of his own, he was well-known for being antifamily. His priorities began and ended with Paxton, and he expected his employees to have the same love and dedication for his company that he did.

Isaac was certain that if Sterling found out about his children, he could pretty much kiss the partnership goodbye.

Needless to say, he was praying his children wouldn't get seriously ill. Although he was already very wealthy and had private insurance coverage, depending on the injury or severity of illness, he could end up in a financial bind. After growing up poor, that was something he never wanted to experience again.

Isaac pushed himself away from the table and rose. "Let's get this show on the road."

He strode to the door and leaned against the wall, waiting while Autumn gathered the rest of her things. Everything she did—straightening the papers, stowing her pen in her purse and then hitching it over her thin shoulder—seemed larger than normal in his eyes.

But of course it wasn't.

It was only him, without understanding his need, trying to soak in as much detail about her as he could, as mundane as it might be. Before he had to turn her loose and go on about his business.

Although he knew he shouldn't, he couldn't stop his eyes from wandering all over her slender body, from tip to toe, as she walked over to him, clasping the thick wad of paperwork in her arms like an innocent schoolgirl. Her curly mane beckoned him unknowingly, her body forcing him to bite the inside of his mouth as he stiffened once again.

"Ready to go?" she asked.

Thank God she was standing an arm's length away, because if he could have it his way that stupid paperwork would be littering the floor and she'd be wrapped in his embrace.

At just over six feet, he was taller than her, yet he knew instinctively she'd be a perfect fit.

"Yeah," he muttered thickly, hoping she couldn't see or hear his desire for her.

He opened the door, bowing slightly. "After you."

She murmured her thanks, giving him a strange smile as she walked out of the room. The sultry way Autumn's skirt clung to her backside was almost too much for one man to bear, especially on a Monday morning.

He'd just turned off the lights in the conference room when his phone rang.

"Hi, Sterling, what can I do for you?"

As he listened to his boss and the man that was almost a father figure to him, his heart raced with excitement and dread.

He ended the call and glanced quickly at Autumn.

"I'm going to need to postpone the tour. Are you going to be okay?"

Her brows knit together in confusion. "What was that about?"

"I'll explain at lunch," he replied, shoving the phone in his pocket. "Meet me in my office at noon."

Without waiting for Autumn's response, he turned and jogged down the hall, feeling her eyes on his back and her smile settling in his heart.

Chapter 3

"And we're off," Autumn whispered under her breath as she watched Isaac round the corner.

Way to go, Sterling.

Her plan was falling together nicely. Though she was curious what her new boss had said on the phone to make Isaac invite her to lunch, it hardly mattered. She routinely left the initial minor details of a surveillance case up to the client. Experience taught her that doing so put her on the fast track to gaining her client's trust. In the end, she did what she wanted, when she wanted to do it, whether the client liked it or not. All was forgiven when she solved a case and got the answers they wanted.

Autumn shifted the stack of papers in her hand, wishing she could toss them into the nearest trash can.

She had no need for any of the Paxton benefits, the government took care of her quite nicely. Whether she had a nosebleed or a gunshot wound, she could walk, run or crawl to any hospital and get medical help. No questions asked and no payment required. Being a friend of Uncle Sam was the best insurance policy in the nation.

Hopefully neither of those injuries would occur on this case. But Autumn wasn't so sure about what would happen to her heart. Over the past few years, she'd been in some pretty scary situations, but none of them made her heart beat as hard as it did when she looked at Isaac, or when he looked at her.

The raw power that he exuded, even when he was relaxed, made her unabashedly wet between the legs.

She smiled with pleasure. It wasn't until the end of the meeting, when she had stood before him and his hot gaze sent a jolt of fire down her body, that she'd realized his hunger was for her.

Sadly, she'd almost laughed. The man had no idea that she was there to potentially destroy him.

It had been a while since she'd seen that look in a man's eyes, and even longer since she'd welcomed it.

But Isaac? He was different. If she were to be truly honest with herself, there was something about Isaac that made her want to run into his arms. Yet, for the good of the case, she knew she would do well to remind herself on a daily basis that she was there to learn the truth, not hop into bed with the most gorgeous man she'd seen since—well…ever.

What she needed right now was a distraction. A nice

cup of tea would make her forget about Isaac's tawny-brown eyes and help her refocus on the investigation.

She was just about to try to find the Paxton cafeteria herself when she heard a voice calling her name. She turned to see Felicia walking toward her. How she didn't manage to trip in those stiletto heels was an unfortunate miracle in itself.

"There you are. I've been looking all over for you, and here you are exactly where I left you."

Felicia's voice was so syrupy sweet that it made Autumn want to gag.

She opened the door to the conference room, peered inside and quickly shut it. "Where's Isaac?" she demanded.

Autumn pasted a smile on her face. "He had to run to a meeting."

"You mean he left you here without giving you a tour?"

"No. He gave me the tour," she lied. "We stopped back at the conference room because I accidentally left my paperwork on the table."

Autumn grasped the wad and waved it in Felicia's face so hard her eyes blinked. "See?"

Felicia pushed the paper away with annoyance. "All I see is that it's not filled out. You'd better get to your desk and get started."

"Sure. I would be happy to do so if I knew where my desk was located."

Felicia touched the back of her hair. "All analysts are housed in the cubicles on the second floor. Didn't Isaac show you?" she said impatiently.

Autumn shook her head. "No, that was our last stop but then he was suddenly called into a meeting."

Felicia let out an exasperated breath. "Come on, I'll show you." She started down the hall, muttering under her breath. "I guess if you want something done right around here, you've got to do it yourself."

"Wait," Autumn called out. "Sterling wrote down the location of my work space. He said it was somewhere on this floor."

Felicia swiveled on her heels, her eyes narrowing. "Are you sure? This floor is for members of the Paxton executive team only."

Autumn accidentally dropped the scrap of paper Sterling had given her earlier. She bent to retrieve it and when she stood, Felicia rudely snatched it away.

"Let me see that." Felicia's cheeks reddened and she crumpled the paper into a ball.

Autumn bit back a smile. She had no idea where her work space was located, but it was obvious the woman didn't like it.

They walked down the carpeted hallway, in the opposite direction from where Isaac had run, and through a small corridor. A few minutes later, they stopped in front of a door with no nameplate. It was constructed of heavy wood and there was a thin plane of glass running vertically down one side of the door, the view through which was obstructed by cardboard.

"I think my father has made a mistake. We use this room for file storage."

Felicia's hand shook a little as she placed it on the knob and turned. "I don't understand this," she shrieked.

Autumn stepped into the small but clean room. Two rusty gray file cabinets lined one wall, one of which was graced with a plastic houseplant that had lost most of its leaves. The old-fashioned metal desk had a couple of beat-up chairs in front of it. On the desk was one of those spotlight lamps, the kind with the lightbulb that burned so hot it could singe anything that got to close to it.

Clearly, the room had been hastily furnished with some vintage finds from somebody's attic or basement. A laptop was the only modern thing in the whole place.

Autumn walked around the desk and set down the stack of papers she was lugging around, as well as her purse. Then she sat in the vintage wooden chair and spun around to face Felicia, who was still by the door.

"It's perfect!" she exclaimed with a broad smile. "What's wrong with it?"

"It's…it's…*ugly,*" Felicia sputtered. "The furnishings are horrendous, not at all what we have in the other offices. Not to mention the fact that this is a file room and no one but me is supposed to be in here."

Felicia looked out into the hallway before she moved deeper inside the room and looked around. "But where are all the *files?*" she wailed, her eyes wide to the whites. "This room was nearly filled with boxes and now there are only about half left."

Hopefully, only the ones I need for the investigation, Autumn thought, snickering inwardly.

Sterling may be a grump, but he was turning out to be very, very handy.

Felicia walked up to the desk and planted her hands

on her hips. "I'm sure this is only a temporary office," she said with a note of derision. "There must be some issue with getting your cubicle ready on the second floor. I'll speak to my father and we'll get this matter straightened out right away."

Autumn nodded and tugged on the middle drawer of her desk. "Sounds good." The drawer stuck, so she tugged even harder and when she finally managed to pull it open, the metal on metal scraped together so loudly that Felicia covered her ears.

The drawer was well stocked with office supplies. Another plus for Sterling. She grabbed the first pen she saw and quickly uncapped it. "I'll get started on that paperwork now and will have it to you by lunch, okay?"

"Fine," Felicia snapped, looking over her shoulder again, as if she was expecting someone. "I should have this work space issue corrected by then."

Autumn rose and went to the door, feigning eagerness to finally start her first day on the job, in the hopes that Felicia would leave. "Thanks for all your help. I'll drop by your office in a couple of hours."

She leaned against the jamb and watched as Felicia suddenly hurried down the hall as fast as her stiletto heels could take her. The woman seemed genuinely distraught and confused about the whole situation. She was about to shut the door when she looked up and suddenly realized why.

Isaac Mason's office was directly opposite hers.

Isaac smoothed one hand over his close-cropped hair and then got to work reknotting his tie. It was almost noon and he'd made it through his morning meetings, his clients were happy, and there were no frantic phone calls from his children.

Like one of his favorite rappers once said, "It's been a good day." But Isaac knew it was long from over.

He wasn't happy about what Sterling had asked him to do, but if he wanted to make partner, he had no choice.

With his tie neatened to his satisfaction, he took one last glance in the mirror, ignoring the rumble in his belly and hammering of his heart.

It's just lunch, he told himself, and Autumn's just another coworker. But he knew she was more than that, or at least he wished she could be.

Isaac walked over to his desk and password-protected his computer. After glancing out his office window, he opened the door and was shrugging into his coat when Autumn stepped out of the opposite office.

"Well, hello!" she greeted him.

Isaac pulled on the lapels of his coat. "What are you doing in there?" he asked, pointing his finger at the closed door. "That's the file room."

She gave him a cheery smile. "It's my office now."

Before he could ask any more questions, she started to walk away.

"Where are we going to lunch? The cafeteria? Because I'm starved."

The thought of food was distracting enough without having to watch her sumptuous bottom sway down the hall and not be able to cradle it in his hands. During his morning meetings, his mind had wandered into random thoughts of her—a kind of subtle curiosity that would only be satisfied by seeing and feeling this woman who could never be his, except in his dreams.

"Um. N-no," he stuttered, feeling a little like Clark Kent chasing Lois as he quickly moved beside her. "I thought we'd go somewhere a little quieter. I have something I need to talk to you about."

"Sounds serious. Is everything all right?"

"No, but it will be."

It has to be, Isaac thought. He had to find a way to get back into Sterling's good graces again. If he could pull this off, he'd make partner for sure.

He leaned against the wall as they waited for the elevator and admired the clean lines of the soft gray coat she wore. Tailored at the waist, it accentuated her trim figure and ended midthigh, which suited him just fine. The more leg she revealed the better, and from where he stood, Lord knows she had two mighty fine ones.

Damn.

There were thousands of women in New York, and the only one that had piqued his interest was off-limits and off-the-chain gorgeous.

Isaac cleared his throat and turned away before his lower body gave away his thoughts.

"It was snowing earlier. Better button up."

Autumn nodded. "Good idea."

Except for the occasional screech from the elevator cables, they rode down in silence until Autumn started to giggle.

He shifted his feet. "What's so funny?"

Autumn pressed her lips together and finished buttoning her coat. "I was just remembering the look on Felicia's face when she saw I had the office opposite yours. She was so pissed. I wonder why?"

Isaac knew why, but he wasn't about to say anything. It was embarrassing enough how Felicia had thrown herself at him, luring him into that very room, where she was hidden among the boxes, stark naked.

He shuddered at the memory. Although he didn't have a type, per se, Felicia definitely wasn't it.

Now Autumn, on the other hand, was a different story. He'd only met her a few hours ago and already he was entertaining fantasies of a hot and heavy office romance. Whether this sudden lust was the result of a lack of coffee, fumes of sleep or zero sex, he couldn't pinpoint. But if it involved two hearts possibly getting broken, one of them being his, he wasn't about to take the risk.

The cold January air was like a rude slap in the face as they walked out of the Paxton Building. The winds didn't help, either. The weatherman that morning had said they were blowing out of the northeast, but they felt like they were from Antarctica and their new home was in the bones of everyone who had ventured outside.

"Wh-where are we headed? I—I'm freezing already!" Autumn ground out through chattering teeth.

Isaac pulled up the collar of his black wool coat. "Not far, just a few blocks."

They joined the throng of people huddled against the chill and walked south, passing a variety of street vendors braving the cold and selling gloves, hats and scarves plastered with "NYC."

"Toasties! Toasties! Two for a dollar," cried one enterprising man. His West African lilt was as welcome as the little hand warmers he was selling.

Isaac stopped and bought four of them. He gave the guy a fifty-dollar bill and told him to keep the change.

"For the way back," he said, giving a pair to Autumn.

He wished he could warm up her hands in his own way, but these would have to do.

Her grateful smile was all the warmth he needed. He'd almost forgotten how nice it felt to give to someone other than his children.

"Thanks. This wind is a killer. I forgot my gloves this morning. First-day jitters, I guess."

A minute later, they arrived at Le Jardin Rouge, a popular Wall Street restaurant that was anything but French. As soon as they walked in, the din and clamor of spirited conversation floated around them.

Autumn looked around and Isaac could tell she wanted to cover her ears.

"You call this quiet?"

Isaac held up his hand as a waiter approached with a couple of menus.

"Mr. Mason, hello again. I have your regular table."

He led them through a narrow hallway, past the kitchen, to a single room in the back.

Inside was a linen-covered table with two chairs and a fire roaring in the fireplace. They hung their coats on the two porcelain-tipped hooks on the wall and sat down.

"Thanks, Eric. Give us a moment, will you?"

After the waiter left, Isaac smiled and handed Autumn her menu.

"All better?" he asked, gesturing toward the low flames roaring in the fireplace.

Autumn nodded and moved her chair into place. "Much. And I can barely hear the other customers all the way back here."

"Yes, I often bring clients by for lunch or when I need to get away from the office, I just come here by myself and work. It's got a ton of character, no?"

"It's lovely!" Autumn rubbed her hands together in front of the fire. "What's good here?"

"Everything, mostly. The butternut squash soup is my favorite, especially on a chilly day like today. It'll help warm us both up."

The waiter entered the room with two bottles of mineral water. Isaac ordered the soups and a couple of side salads.

"That was awesome what you did back there," Autumn remarked, unfolding her napkin. "For me and for that vendor."

She poured her water into her glass and took a sip. "And here I thought all men who worked on Wall Street were ruthless penny-pinchers."

Isaac felt the blood rush to the tips of his ears, something that happened whenever he was either very embarrassed or very angry. In this case, her compliment pleased him, but he merely shrugged.

He squeezed a lemon into his water. "Contrary to popular belief, I can be a nice guy. But in order to make money in this town, one can't be afraid to push past boundaries and take risks."

"Even when it involves breaking the law?"

Her question wasn't posed in an accusatory tone. Still, it was unsettling and left a metallic taste in his mouth. Isaac was glad when the waiter approached the table with a basket of bread and their salads.

When they were alone again, Isaac asked, "Have you ever heard of the saying 'Whoever controls the money makes the rules?'"

Autumn buttered her bread and nodded.

He took a deep breath. "Sometimes it's true."

And he was living it. Or at least he used to...

The meetings to which he was mysteriously not invited, the silence that often befell a room whenever he walked in, and the opportunities for new client business that lately seemed to go to someone else or he never even heard about in the first place.

He was the wealthiest senior investment banker on staff. In fact, he made more money in his yearly bonuses than in his regular salary. But, lately, it seemed as if everyone was treating him like some runny-nosed intern.

Isaac kept thinking the cold-shoulder treatment from Sterling and the other staff was because he was being groomed for the responsibilities of becoming an executive partner, where there was less day-to-day trading and managing clients and more focus on higher-level investment strategy for the firm overall.

There was something wrong going on at Paxton, something he didn't understand, but he wasn't ready to believe that the something wrong could be him.

"So are you saying it's okay to look the other way?" Autumn pressed. Her brown eyes seemed as intense as the flames warming the room.

"Sometimes," he cautioned. Autumn's eyes narrowed almost imperceptibly and she seemed disappointed with his answer. "But only until one is sure that pursuing it means a net gain for both parties," he added, not wanting to upset her.

Autumn rolled her eyes and speared a piece of romaine. "You sound like one of my old bosses. Every question I asked the guy, the answer he would give me would sound like it came out of a textbook for Economics 101."

Isaac laughed, almost spitting out the water he was in the middle of drinking.

"I'm that bad, huh?"

Autumn munched on her salad and nodded.

"In that case, maybe I should quit investment banking and become a professor."

She swallowed and pointed her fork at him. "Maybe you should," she advised, her tone serious. "But not before you tell me why you invited me to lunch."

Autumn pursed her lips into a pouty smile that nearly teased him to distraction, and he realized that he felt so comfortable with her that he'd nearly forgotten the reason he'd invited her to the restaurant in the first place.

"Ah yes," he said, as the waiter arrived with two steaming bowls of soup. "We have an assignment."

"What do you mean by 'we'?" Autumn asked. "I thought you said that the analysts and investment and trading guys never worked together. Something about conflict of interest?"

Isaac nodded. "We usually don't. But this assignment came direct from Sterling, so I don't ask questions. He must have his reasons for wanting to do it this way."

She blew on her spoon and swallowed some soup. "Mmm…this is delicious. Okay, so what do we need to do?"

Isaac ate a few spoonfuls of soup and wiped his mouth with his napkin. "Have you ever heard of Eleanor Witterman?"

"Sure. She's a New York City legend. The wealthy socialite who never married. She's had plenty of suitors, or so they say. How old is she now?"

Isaac thought a moment. "Late fifties, early sixties maybe? She's around the same age as Sterling. But from the photos I've seen, she doesn't look it at all."

Autumn twisted her lips to the side. "She must have her plastic surgeon on speed dial," she remarked. "What about her?"

He smiled and took a sip of water before continuing. "Sterling has been trying to get her to become a client for years, but she's never come on board. Seems lately she's had a change of heart. Recently she sold a large portion of her art collection for just over ten million dollars, and she came to Paxton seeking counsel on how to invest it."

Autumn's eyes widened. "That's great. Any reason why she sold all that art?"

Isaac shrugged and leaned back in his chair.

"Who cares?" he said with a smile. "We've got ten million dollars to play with!"

"Where do I fit in this game of real-life monopoly?"

"You and I are going to put together an investment package that Eleanor won't be able to resist."

"That sounds more up your alley than mine. I'm an analyst, remember? I'm the one who double-checks all the calculations making sure one plus two doesn't equal four."

"Right, but to get this deal, we're going to need your forecasting and predictive analysis skills, as well."

"You mean you want me to be a fortune teller?" Autumn replied drily. She grabbed her purse and pretended to be searching for something. "Nope, no crystal ball in here."

"Come on, Autumn. You know everyone on Wall Street relies on a little wizardry now and then."

"Which is why we've had a financial meltdown in the United States and around the world," she retorted, folding her arms.

Isaac's mouth dropped open. He hadn't expected any push back, especially from a new employee. Maybe he'd been wrong about Autumn. Sterling was obviously losing his Midas touch in terms of hiring suitable Paxtonites.

"Whose side are you on, anyway?"

He tossed his napkin on the table and gave her a pointed stare. "You work in this industry. You know the way things are. Millions of stocks are traded every day by computer algorithms, not people. It's the new world order."

Autumn held up her hands. "I realize that, okay? All I'm saying is that we all should take some responsibility for what goes on, and what goes wrong, in our industry."

Isaac felt the tips of his ears get hot; and this time he wasn't happy. This lunch meeting was not turning out the way he expected. Autumn was looking like she would be difficult to work with, and yet, he had no choice.

He leaned forward and said in a hard voice, "The only responsibility I care about right now is the one I have to Paxton. And as a new member of our team, I would have thought you'd have a better attitude about this assignment."

Autumn's eyes widened. "I'm sorry, Isaac," she said, frowning. "Sometimes I just get caught up in all the negativity that surrounds our industry that I lose sight of all the good, and I know Paxton is one of the good guys."

She swiped at her left eye with one finger and Isaac wasn't sure if she was removing a tear or a speck of dust. No way could he have a woman crying because of him.

That would not be a very good day.

He paid for the meal in cash and they retrieved their coats. He waited until they were outside until he spoke again. The mood between them, which had been friendly an hour ago, was as icy as the air.

"Look, Autumn, let me give you the lowdown on Eleanor," he said, softening his voice. "She's very old-fashioned. She doesn't want her money being handled by computers, but by real people. Any investments we advise are going to be backed up by real numbers, forecasted to predict the dividends she could expect to receive in x number of years."

Autumn nodded, looking contrite, and for a moment he felt guilty for getting so angry at her.

She tilted her chin, and he noticed she had a tiny mole on her jawline. "When do we get started?"

"Immediately. The presentation is in two weeks. I want you to begin looking into possibilities this afternoon. I have a full day of meetings tomorrow, so if you're available, I'd like to have an early dinner so we can review your initial recommendations."

Autumn buttoned up her coat. "There are hundreds of industries or companies she could possibly invest in. Any idea where to start?"

Isaac thought a moment. "How about with her best friends?"

Autumn gave him a quizzical smile. "And who might they be?"

"Diamonds."

She burst out in a deep, knowing laugh, which was definitely better than almost making her cry.

He wiggled his fingers at her. "Now let's bust open these hand warmers and get back to the office. We both have a lot of work to do."

As they walked back, hands stuffed deep in their coat pockets against the harsh January winds, Isaac knew the hardest part of the days and nights ahead would be trying to stop Autumn from getting under his skin, or into his heart.

Chapter 4

When they got back to Paxton, Autumn stopped at the restroom to freshen up. Just as she suspected, the tears she'd nearly unloaded on Isaac had taken a toll on her mascara. Of course, they weren't real. She'd only pretended that she was going to cry.

Deep down she hated to use such a manipulative trick, but it was the only way she knew how to get a sense of his character.

She wet a paper towel and dabbed at her eyelashes. When she was finished, she smiled at her reflection in the mirror. Thank goodness, Isaac had passed her test.

He cared.

She was impressed with how well he treated the street vendor and their waiter at the restaurant. He didn't have to give either man any extra change or tips, but he did.

And he didn't have to care whether her hands were cold, either. Her heart swelled remembering how he'd bought her the hand warmers. She couldn't remember the last time someone had done something so sweet for her, just to save her from discomfort.

And she was relieved because maybe, just maybe, he wasn't like all the other greedy, stingy, emotionally dead men she'd met—and busted—while working undercover.

In her experience, the maxim "the bigger the bank account, the larger the ego" was a reality. There was something about making a ton of money that made some men turn into arrogant egomaniacs who thought they were above the law.

It was true that Isaac didn't seem to be too concerned about how Wall Street sometimes negatively affected Main Streets all around the world. He was likely worried about his job, and rightly so; otherwise, Sterling wouldn't have hired her to investigate him.

If he didn't have the activist mentality that she did, perhaps it was because he truly believed he wasn't doing anything wrong. Autumn hoped that's what she would discover, too. All she had to do was remember to avoid letting her emotions get in the way of her case.

When she got back to her office, Isaac's door was open, but he wasn't there. Presumably, he was already well into his afternoon meetings.

She hung up her coat, walked to the desk and noticed a light blinking on her phone.

Oh joy, she thought, her first voice mail.

Twenty minutes later, she'd figured out how to retrieve the message. It was Sterling calling for an update. The man certainly didn't waste any time, she mused while locking her purse in her desk. Although she wasn't particularly afraid it would get stolen, she wasn't stupid.

Petty crimes in the workplace were a common occurrence—a box of binder clips here, a laptop there. She wasn't about to give anyone the rope of temptation. Plus, the location of her office was a little remote, which was likely the reason it was originally used for storage.

Autumn grabbed a pen and an index pad and headed down to Sterling's office. His secretary, Doris, a plump woman who somehow managed to look attractive even with a tiny gap in her front teeth, informed Autumn that Sterling was on a call and she would have to wait.

Ten minutes later, the woman ushered her into his office and Autumn almost burst out laughing when she tiptoed out. But when she saw Sterling's face, she knew why. The man looked like he could melt copper off a penny with his eyes alone.

She took a few, tentative steps toward his desk. "I got your voice mail. You wanted to see me?"

Sterling motioned her closer, waving his hands impatiently.

"Yes, yes. Come in."

Autumn parked herself in one of the maroon-tufted leather chairs fronting Sterling's enormous desk.

She gave him her sweetest smile. "Is there anything wrong?"

"The world's gone to hell, that's all," he barked, and

sat down hard. "I'm hoping you have some good news for me. What have you learned so far?"

That Isaac was as kind as he was cute, she thought, but she knew that wasn't the information Sterling was seeking.

"Not much yet," she admitted. "We went to lunch and he informed me of our assignment."

"And what do you think?"

"It's brilliant."

"I know," Sterling replied. "I thought of it, didn't I?"

Autumn wanted to gag at the air of superiority in his tone, but at least his eyes didn't have daggers in them anymore.

"You certainly did, and it's the perfect way for me to observe how Isaac prepares for a new client presentation from start to finish."

Sterling steepled his fingers. "I called you in here because I want you to know that this is a real assignment with a real client, not a decoy."

Autumn nodded. "I'm glad you told me. I was kind of wondering about that when Isaac indicated the client seems to be afraid of computers."

"Eleanor Witterman is not afraid of computers," Sterling corrected. "She simply doesn't trust them. Quite frankly, on days like today, I think she might be right."

Autumn raised an eyebrow, not knowing what he meant but gathering it had something to do with the world going to hell.

"Don't worry, Mr. Paxton. I'll do my best to make every investment we advise as transparent as possible."

"Good," he replied with a satisfied nod. "How do you like your office?"

"It's great. Nice touch on the old office furniture. Very film noir. I feel like Jimmy Cagney's going to show up at any second and offer me a cigar."

He snorted a laugh. The sound was like a street full of taxis honking in unison. "Yeah. I picked it out myself. Straight from the storage closet in the basement. My father started this business back in the early 1950s and he was something of a pack rat."

"Are the boxes in my office the files you want me to review?"

Sterling nodded, absently jingling the coins in his pocket. "There are about eight years of records contained in those files. The rest are electronic."

"And these are all the deals Isaac has been involved with since he's been employed here?"

"Yes. He interned here while he was an undergrad, and then I hired him full-time after he graduated from Harvard."

"What made you think he'd be a good fit for Paxton?"

"He's smart. Smarter than a lot of people around here initially gave him credit for."

She gave him a pointed stare. "Why? Because he's black?"

Yeah. I went there, Autumn thought as Sterling sat up in his chair, his pale face aghast.

"We don't condone, nor will we tolerate, any form of discrimination here at Paxton."

She thinned her lips and didn't back down. In order

to conduct her investigation, she needed to have all the facts. Even the ugly ones.

"However since you asked," Sterling relented with a shrug. "That could have been the reason initially, but it's certainly not the case now."

His broad smile should have been reassuring, but instead it made Autumn wonder if he was telling her the truth.

Sterling reached for his phone, effectively ending the meeting. "Please keep me posted on any new developments," he ordered in a brusque tone. By the time she shut the door, he was already engaged in another heated discussion. She flashed a sympathetic smile at his secretary and headed back to her own office.

Isaac's door was now closed. He had the little strip of glass next to his door, too, but she wasn't about to peek in and see if he was there. She did, however, take a moment to peel away the cardboard from the glass in her own office. Not only was it tacky, but she didn't want to appear as if she had something to hide.

Autumn shut the door and sat down at her desk, rubbing at her pulsating temples, a sure sign a headache was in the works.

Sterling seemed appeased for now, but he'd want action quickly. While she was eager to get started, she was also afraid that she wouldn't like the answers she found.

The first thing Autumn needed to do was access Isaac's files on the network.

She couldn't help feeling slightly disappointed that Sterling had sent the security credentials via email. Hacking into Paxton's computer system was infinitely more fun and challenging, but time was not on her side. With only weeks to complete her investigation, the pressure from Sterling to wrap things up quickly was real.

As she waited for her computer to boot up, she dug out two ibuprofen and a bottle of water from her tote bag. She washed down the pills and was just about to open up her email when there were three sharp raps on the door.

Her heart beat faster, and she hoped it was Isaac coming to check in on her. She spun around, trying to catch her reflection in the window, but all she saw was snow. Facing the door, she quickly smoothed her errant curls, praying she didn't look like she'd just stuck her finger in a light socket.

"Come in!"

Felicia sauntered in and put her hands on hips. "You'll be happy to know you're staying right here."

Autumn felt her headache immediately worsen, noting that Felicia looked anything but happy. The scowl on her face could make a clown cry.

"I've checked with my father and it seems he was the one who arranged everything, without clearing it with me."

"I'm sorry there was a misunderstanding," Autumn said, under the woman's glare. "Thank you for clearing it up."

Felicia gestured toward the brown boxes lining the floor, dismissing Autumn's apology. "And these are supposed to remain here, although I don't know what for, but Daddy instructed me not to remove them."

"Were you able to locate the other boxes that were here?"

"Of course I did," Felicia snapped. "And they are now in an undisclosed location."

Felicia glanced at the boxes again and her brow creased, which made Autumn wonder why she was so concerned about the dusty, old files.

"I think the reason those are staying is because Isaac and I are working together on an important new business presentation," Autumn offered, trying to distract her. "He wants me to review previous history to get me acclimated to the way things are done around here."

Felicia turned and gave her a smile that Autumn knew was not meant to be friendly.

"Sterling told me about the assignment, which is why you're in here, in this cozy little office, and not down there on the farm," she said, referring to the floor where all the other analysts worked in tiny cubicles.

Autumn noted that Felicia didn't add "where you belong" to the end of her statement, but she got the gist. The executive floor was her territory and Autumn wasn't welcome.

Still, Autumn knew she had to do something to appease her; otherwise, Felicia could become a hindrance to her investigation, like a cockroach she could never kill.

She pushed away from her desk and crossed her legs.

"Somehow it seems we've gotten off to a bad start, and I just want you to know that if you ever need anything, I'm here."

Felicia tilted her head, and a few blond strands wafted around her face, softening her appearance.

"That's very kind of you, so I'll offer you one piece of advice."

"What's that?" Autumn asked, thinking she was going to tell her that short-term disability insurance was a good investment.

Felicia glanced behind her shoulder and turned back. "Watch out for Isaac. He has a reputation around here that's not as glowing as you might think."

Autumn wanted to tell Felicia that talking about a fellow employee behind his back had to be against the human resources official code of conduct, but she remained silent. It wouldn't do her any good to invoke Felicia's wrath when, at some point in the future, she could prove to be useful for something other than idle gossip.

"Don't let his looks or his money fool you," Felicia added before walking out.

"And don't let the door hit you in the ass," Autumn muttered under her breath.

God, the woman was infuriating.

No doubt Felicia was outside peeking in Isaac's little window to see if he was there. Her warning about him didn't ring any serious alarm bells for now, although it did make Autumn question Felicia's motive for telling her. She made a mental note to closely observe any future interactions between the two.

After downing the last of her water, she opened her email.

The first was from Sterling and contained the credentials for the network, plus his cell phone number with instructions telling her he was available 24/7 for any updates.

While she appreciated his eagerness, this was a potential case of corporate fraud, not murder, and she hoped there wouldn't be a need for a late-night phone call. If the man sounded like he wanted to smash heads at one in the afternoon, she shuddered to think what he'd sound like at three in the morning.

The second email was from Isaac.

Lunch was fun. I look forward to working with you on the Witterman pitch.

Since we're on such a tight time frame, please feel free to call my cell at any time if you have questions or concerns.

—Isaac

Autumn's lips turned up in a smile as she programmed his number into her cell, thinking she would call just to hear his voice. She suspected his playful tenor could turn passionate with the right woman.

She closed her eyes as a part of her wished she could be that woman. The part that missed a man's awakening touch, his urgent plea between her thighs, the hush of early-morning loving and the tender kisses that would sustain her all day.

Opening her eyes, she leaned her elbows on the desk and put her hands against her flushed cheeks. Daydreaming about Isaac being the one who could lift her self-imposed ban on men meant that she needed to get back to work.

She glanced over at the boxes in the corner and wondered why she dreaded reviewing them all. She was a natural snoop, so normally she didn't mind digging through reams of paperwork and finding the evidence she needed to help bring about justice.

But this case was different because she didn't want to find out anything bad about Isaac.

Even though she didn't know him, when she looked into his eyes, something deep inside her only wanted to see the good. The complete opposite of what she was called to do as a private investigator. To uphold the law, she had to condemn.

With a sigh, she decided she would take a stack of files home every night where she could review them while drinking a nice, big glass of wine.

She turned her attention back to the case by researching Paxton's prospective client, Eleanor Witterman. The search netted a surprising number of results for the never-married socialite.

Most were news items about the recent sale of her art collection, which consisted primarily of works by French painters such as Degas, Monet, Renoir and others whose last names sounded equally romantic.

There was also an article where she admitted she was something of a Francophile, a person who just can't get enough of all things French, including in her own words "Frenchmen." And while she'd reflected she'd had many lovers, no one could make her forget the one who broke her heart.

I'm not rich, but at least my heart is intact.

Autumn counted herself among the lucky ones. She'd

never had her heart broken, likely because she never let anyone get close enough to have the chance.

In Isaac's case, she knew she had to keep her lucky streak going, not that he gave her any outward, public displays of interest. Although a few times today at lunch, she did catch him glancing at her as if he wished he could.

In his eyes, the desire was there. But so was the wall.

At least they had those two things in common.

Autumn redirected herself back to beginning her analysis of the investment market for diamonds.

Prior to bringing one company to its knees for securities fraud and before she started working as a private investigator, she was primarily involved in researching stocks and bonds. So she was surprised to learn that diamonds had outperformed equities in recent years. The risks were a market that was complex, unregulated and highly secretive. Certainly not advisable for the average investor, but for a woman with Eleanor's wealth, investing in the diamond market might make sense.

Still, it was important for any investor to have a balanced portfolio and Autumn knew she had a ton of research ahead of her so that she could make the best investment recommendations.

Although she thought it was odd that Isaac didn't suggest a discovery meeting with Eleanor so they could get a better understanding of her risk potential, that was really his call. She had no choice but to trust that he had his reasons for moving forward.

She glanced at her watch and saw that it was nearly five o'clock. She'd better get moving if she was going to leave the office before Isaac. It wouldn't do for him to discover that she lived in the same building as he did. In a city of eight million people, it was the best way to keep tabs on him, plus the view of Central Park was fabulous.

Autumn got up and walked over to the boxes. She knelt down for a closer look and was glad to see they were organized by year. She opened up the oldest one and selected as many files as she could hold in one hand, before standing up and stuffing them into her tote bag.

After packing up her laptop and fetching her purse, she buttoned her coat, cracked open the door slightly and frowned. Isaac's door was shut and the lights were off.

Her brow crinkled. When had he left for the day? She hadn't heard any sounds in the hallway.

She guessed it was because diamonds had a way of commanding her complete attention. Or maybe she was just trying to let herself off the hook, she chided herself and vowed to be more observant of Isaac tomorrow. She certainly didn't need any excuses to keep a close eye on his beautiful body.

Worried that Isaac would be standing at the elevators, she shut her door and leaned against it to wait for a few minutes, trying not to be upset that he didn't say goodbye.

Isaac heaved his backpack over his shoulder, trying to ignore all the work within it. He picked up the pizza from the counter, pushed open the door and joined the swarm of people on Madison Avenue.

Eager to get home to his children, he walked as quickly as he could through meandering tourists and hurried workers rushing to get to the subway. Thankfully, the ice on the sidewalk had melted, but with the temperature dropping again that evening, he knew it would be treacherous in the morning.

When he arrived at his building, he glanced up at the evergreen cloth awning with amusement. The name of his apartment building was The Staffordshire, a name he always thought was better suited to a country estate in England than a high-rise apartment building in New York City. Central Park was right across the street, so he supposed that counted as the "country," and although he owned his apartment, with the maintenance fees he was paying every year, he could have bought an estate fit for a king a long time ago.

Isaac nodded to the doorman, got in the elevator, punched in his code and rode to the penthouse level.

When he arrived, the apartment was oddly silent. Normally when he got home, the television was on and his children were plopped in front of it, zoned out like two zombies.

"Anybody home?" he called, setting his backpack on the floor. When he didn't get an answer, he walked into the kitchen and yelled, "I've got pizza!"

Like magic, his children materialized.

Devon, his twelve-year-old son, ran and slid into the room in his sock feet. His sixteen-year-old daughter, Deshauna, entered a few moments later with the unhurried saunter so typical of teenagers.

That five-letter word works every time, he thought.

"Hey, guys! I've got your favorite." He opened and presented the box with as much flair as he could muster. "Pepperoni, broccoli and onions!"

Deshauna took out her earbuds and made a face. "Um…the broccoli-and-onions part? That's your favorite, Dad."

"Yeah. I hate broccoli," Devon joined in. "But I like the onions. They're slimy and go down like worms," he added, rubbing his stomach with a satisfied grin.

"Eww, get a life, Devon."

Feeling an argument was about to ensue, Isaac quickly closed the pizza box and set it on the granite countertop.

"How about we all grab something to drink from the refrigerator and eat? Devon, you get the plates. Deshauna, you get the napkins and silverware."

While his kids set the table, Isaac made a salad by grabbing a bag of pre-mixed lettuce from the refrigerator and pouring the contents into a bowl. If only everything in life were this easy, he thought as he retrieved a couple of bottles of salad dressing, mentally bracing himself for the latest crisis that his kids faced that day.

Devon and Deshauna had grown up in a slew of foster homes, just like he did, and were having some trouble adjusting to a new, stable life.

He'd adopted them both as he couldn't bear for them not to be together. Although now, Isaac chuckled to himself, he had to break them apart on a daily basis to keep them from killing each other. The struggle to survive had transitioned into sibling rivalry, and he was still trying to figure out how to manage it.

Food was the great equalizer though, and he was glad when they were all sitting down and digging in.

"So," he said, passing the salad, "how was your day?"

"I got an A on my math homework!" Devon said, his lips greasy with pizza sauce.

"That's great. So all that hard work you did last night paid off," Isaac said, resisting the urge to tell Devon to wipe his mouth. A boy should be able to eat his pizza in peace during a moment of glory, right?

It was times like these that he wished he had a wife. She could be the etiquette cop in the household and the kids could blame her for spoiling all the fun, instead of him.

Yes, she'd be mad at him for a while, but he'd be sure to make it up to her in bed all night long.

An image of Autumn suddenly popped into his brain. She was lying in his bed in a sheer lace nightgown and he was kissing the pout off her beautiful face.

Why am I thinking of her now? he wondered, even as he realized he hadn't stopped thinking about her all day.

"What about you, Deshauna? Did you get a chance to talk to the guidance counselor?"

His daughter, who was a junior in high school, was just starting the process of looking at colleges. His heart pinched in his chest, thinking about her going away in less than two years, when he'd just found her.

Deshauna nodded, her bangs falling across her forehead. "I brought a bunch of information home. Some of the papers we need to have back to her by tomorrow. Will you have time tonight?"

Isaac thought about the slew of work in his backpack. It would be another late night, but his kids came first.

"Sure thing, honey. Let's take a look right after dinner."

Her smile quickly turned into a scowl when Devon grabbed another slice of pizza. "Do you have to eat so much?"

"I dunno," Devon shot back. "Do you have to FaceTime with that boy every day after school?"

Isaac stopped chewing and stared at his daughter. "What boy?"

With a mortified look, Deshauna tried to kick her brother under the table, but he scooted away just in time, nearly taking the tablecloth with him.

"Cut it out!" Isaac instructed, inwardly proud that he managed to sound calmer than he really was. Between the two of them, he'd be lucky if he made it to his forties without having a heart attack.

"Deshauna, we'll talk about this later." He piled a second helping of salad on his plate. "Now, why don't one of you ask me about my day?"

"How was your day, Dad?" they chorused.

"So much for following directions," he commented drily. "But since you both asked, it was great. A new employee started working at Paxton today. Her name is Autumn."

"Ooh…is she hot?" Devon said, gnawing on a piece of crust.

Isaac wanted to laugh at the cuteness of his voice, knowing that Devon was trying to sound cool and grown-up, even though he still liked to play with toys.

"She is, indeed," Isaac replied, playing along. "As hot as those spicy French fries you love to eat."

Deshauna smiled sweetly. "Then you should date her, Dad," she advised.

Isaac could hear in her tone of voice that she was not concerned about his love life, but that dating Autumn might keep him out of her business for a while.

He pushed his chair back and stood. "Sorry to disappoint you guys, but I don't date women I work with."

Devon slurped down the rest of his soda. "Why not?"

"The girl would have to quit when you broke up with her, right, Dad?" his sister piped up in a firm voice, drawing Devon's immediate attention. "And I mean, you would never do that and they would never fire you because you make too much money for them, right?"

Isaac leaned his knuckles on the table and looked at his children. He recognized the worried expressions on their faces as fear. No matter how many times he'd told them they were safe, that they wouldn't be thrown out onto the streets, deep down they still didn't believe him. He'd only adopted them a few months ago and he knew it took time to build trust, but it still hurt him to the core.

"Listen. My job is very stable and I would never, ever do anything to jeopardize it, okay?"

Both children looked relieved and Isaac decided to give them some free time before they started their homework.

When they were gone, he washed the dishes and cleaned off the table, his thoughts turning to the workday.

In all his meetings, where the attendees thought

they'd had his complete attention, he'd only been there in body. His mind had been on Autumn. His penis hardened and grew against the counter just thinking about her full lips, gorgeous hair and curvy breasts.

Just a touch. Just a taste. That's all he wanted.

But he knew he was lying to himself. Because if he was lucky enough or stupid enough to try anything with Autumn, he'd only want more.

When the kitchen was clean, he grabbed his backpack and checked his watch as he walked into his study, pleased to see that he still had time to decompress and come up with a reason Sterling needed to assign someone else to work on the Witterman pitch with Autumn.

Thank goodness, his children had made him come to his senses, he thought, before it was too late.

Chapter 5

At six-thirty the next morning, Autumn slipped a one-hundred-dollar bill into the doorman's hand, who tipped his hat and winked. The man had been true to his word, ringing her apartment when Isaac had gone for his daily jog, with no questions asked.

The brochure for The Staffordshire, home to some of New York City's wealthiest individuals, had boasted of the "utmost privacy afforded to its upscale residents." She got into the cab waiting at the curb and laughed.

They paid for secrecy and so did she.

Irony at its finest.

As the taxi wove down Broadway toward the Financial District, she sat back and yawned so loudly the cabbie gave her the evil eye in the rearview mirror. She'd reviewed files late into the night and wasn't used to so little sleep.

Autumn yawned again and rubbed her shoulders, wishing it was Isaac's hands trying to relieve the knots under her skin, instead of hers. But the ride was too bumpy and her hands were too weak, so she gave up. There'd be many more late nights, so she could probably justify hiring a masseur. Preferably a male with abs so tight she could bounce a quarter off them.

Twenty minutes later, she arrived at the Paxton Building. She stopped in the ground floor café for a steaming cup of green tea and made her way to her office, hoping that Felicia wasn't an early bird like her.

Autumn hung up her coat, replaced the files in the box and chose a new stack. She piled them on her desk and powered up her computer, with the plan to review some now so she wouldn't have such a big stack to take home later. It was just after seven so it should be quiet for a while, as the official work day didn't begin until eight o'clock.

She swiveled her chair toward the window to enjoy the view and sip her tea until her computer finished whirring.

The next thing she knew, there was a knock at the door and she woke with a start, realizing that she'd dozed off for a few minutes. Her face reddened with embarrassment and she quickly turned around just before Isaac cracked open the door.

"Good morning." He popped his head into the room. "Mind if I come in?"

At the sound of his voice, her heart beat rapidly, quickly chasing away any lingering drowsiness.

Without waiting for her answer, he left the door open and straddled one of the chairs in front of her desk.

Isaac glanced at her desk. "Looks like you're already pretty busy," he commented. "What time did you get in today?" Autumn's throat went dry. Had the doorman told him about their little deal?

"Just after seven, why?" she answered, pressing a button to wake up the computer. It had gone to sleep, just like her.

He whistled low. "You keep doing that and you're going to make me look bad."

He gave her a wide smile, his teeth as white as the snow that fell outside her office window, and she knew he was joking.

"I'd have to get here at midnight to make you look bad," she teased back.

His languorous smile was an acknowledgment that he knew he looked good, and he was glad that she noticed.

And, my oh my, did she ever.

He wore no suit jacket, so she had a better view of the way his crisp white shirt stretched over his expansive chest. Although he wore an undershirt, she thought she could still see the barest hint of his nipples through the fabric. And his gray tie? Well, that was like a one-way road to pleasure that ended at his belt buckle.

Isaac Mason was looking fine enough that morning to make her want to shut the office door and slam down his trousers.

There were a lot more interesting ways to conduct an investigation than reading a bunch of files.

The picture in her mind was so vivid her loins trembled and she crossed her legs. The friction it caused between her thighs made her stifle a low moan, which she covered up with a series of coughs.

Isaac tipped his chair against the desk. "Are you okay?" He grabbed the cup of tea from her desk and shoved it at her. "Here, drink this."

She nodded, took a sip and almost gagged. "Ugh. Cold!"

The temperature of the liquid doused the flame of desire in her body like a cold shower.

He took it from her hand. "Do you want me to get you another one?"

She stared at him with surprise. "Sure, that would be great. Green tea, no sugar."

"Be right back," Isaac said, before leaping off the chair and heading out of the office.

Autumn shoved the files into a drawer and took out a mirror, praying she didn't have a line of dried drool on her face. Everything was clear, thank goodness, and she carefully reapplied a light coat of lipstick to freshen up. Due to allergies, she never wore much makeup, so her morning routine was easy, especially since there wasn't a man around to hog the bathroom.

She opened up her email and saw that she had a request from Isaac for an eight-o'clock meeting this morning. It had been sent late last night and marked urgent. She had accepted it to clear the message from her inbox when Isaac stepped back into the room.

"Thanks," she said, taking the cup from Isaac. "I just accepted the meeting request you sent and, like magic, you're here!"

She smiled brightly, but Isaac did not return her smile. Instead, he stood in front of her desk, looking uncomfortable. "Listen, the reason I wanted to meet with you this morning is because I'm going to request that Sterling assign someone else to work with you on the Witterman pitch."

Her heart sank. What had gone wrong? Had Sterling decided to pull the investigation for some reason?

Wait a second, she quickly told herself. Isaac just said that he was going to request to be taken off the project. Nothing had been done yet. She still had time to not only find out why Isaac was so skittish but change his mind, as well.

She walked over to the door and leaned against it to shut it. The desire that had ebbed flamed once again as his eyes roamed up her legs all the way to her face like a white-hot spotlight. She curled her toes in her shoes, basking in his admiration, not willing to ignore it, if only for a moment.

Walking toward him, she decided to sit across from him in the other chair, instead of at her desk. She wanted nothing between them that could impede communication. Hopefully, their discussion would lead to information that would help her understand him better. Deep down, she knew that her need to know everything about Isaac Mason had nothing to do with the case and everything to do with her heart.

Crossing her legs, she gestured to the chair.

"Why don't you sit down and relax."

Isaac hesitated for a second, then straddled the chair as he'd done before.

"Tell me what's going on, Isaac. Is it my background that bothers you? I know I've job-hopped a lot, but I promise I'm not going to jump ship on you. I really think Paxton is good fit for me career-wise."

He regarded her for a minute, then shook his head.

"It's not you, it's me."

She wanted to laugh out loud. How many times had she heard that line before, but hearing it on the job was a first.

"What do you mean?" she asked. "Has something happened?"

"Yeah," he replied. His eyes caught hers, dropped down to her lips, and suddenly she knew.

She put her fingers to her mouth in shock.

"Don't do that," he commanded. "It only makes me want to kiss you more."

He reached for her fingers and clasped them in his hand, and it was warm and strong and rough all at the same time. And if their chairs had wheels, she was sure he'd roll her to him, bringing her close enough to feel the heat from his skin.

But both old-fashioned chairs stayed stolidly on the ground, while her heart pumped so hard that she was sure he could see it right through her sweater.

"I'm more attracted to you than I have a right to be," Isaac admitted, grasping her hand even tighter. "In fact, you're all I've thought about for the last twenty-four hours."

Autumn hitched in a breath at the combination of desire and worry in his voice. She opened her mouth to speak, to tell him that she'd thought of him, too, but she could only tremble.

"That's why I have to ask Sterling to reassign someone else for this pitch."

Isaac leaned in close and ever so slowly brushed his lips along the ridge of her knuckles, daring her with his eyes not to react, not to feel the complexity within that simple caress.

She closed her eyes and tried not to succumb to the river of tingles he was invoking along her skin. But Isaac's lips were so firm, yet gentle and insistent, as they dwelled in those moments upon a part of her hand that she rarely noticed but would never dismiss again.

Autumn heard herself moan softly and it was like a wake-up call she wished she never had. What was wrong with her? She was supposed to be investigating this man, not wanting him to make love to her. She sat back suddenly and Isaac dropped her hand.

"I'm sorry, I—" she sputtered, her head felt as if it was on planet WTF Just Happened.

"Did you enjoy that?" he asked, his tone hopeful, without a touch of ego. "I just had to touch you, and I wanted you to like it. Did you?"

She felt herself nodding. *Oh yes, very much,* she wanted to say, *but the knuckles on my other hand are jealous, can you take care of them, too?*

But instead, she grabbed her tea and shut up. She didn't want to give him any ideas that she hoped he'd take her up on.

"Good."

His smile was kind and it made her insides swoon even more. Then his voice dropped to nearly a whisper.

"Because it can never happen again."

Autumn stood up without looking at him and walked around the desk to the window. She knew what he said was true, but she didn't want to hear him say the words, didn't want to see the need disappear from his eyes.

There was something about a man wanting a woman, a man wanting her, that made a normal, dreary January day seem like summer was right around the corner. And maybe, just maybe, love was there, too.

She could feel his eyes on her back as she pressed her hands against the cold glass. The snow had ceased, leaving only droplets of water that showed a world upside-down.

How could she have lost control so easily?

She'd never given up on an investigation and she wasn't going to start now, no matter the outcome.

Autumn swiveled on her heel and faced him. "You're absolutely right, Isaac, and I agree with your recommendation. I think it will be better for both of us. When are you going to talk with Sterling?"

Isaac stared at her as if he was shocked by her sudden turnaround. He dug his phone out of his pocket and stood.

"In about fifteen minutes."

"Okay. Let me know what happens," she replied, indicating the door with her chin.

He took the hint a few seconds later.

"Guess I'll be having dinner with someone else tonight," she added with a wry smile, and from the look on his face before he shut the door, he didn't like the thought of that at all.

Autumn sank into her office chair and covered her face with her hands. She picked up the phone, with the intent of calling Sterling to warn and advise him how to handle the conversation with Isaac so he wouldn't accidentally blow her cover. The man seemed a bit overwrought, but she decided against it.

Although she didn't want Isaac to leave, the more normal things appeared to him, the better. Otherwise, if she pushed to remain on the Witterman project with him, she feared he might become suspicious. Or worse, he might figure out that she wanted him as much as he wanted her.

Thirty minutes later, she was logged in to the Paxton network, reviewing some of Isaac's most recent deals, when she saw an email notification pop up.

Guess what? You ARE having dinner with me tonight.
Meet me at La Vie at 5:30.
—Isaac

She closed the email and smiled. The plan was still intact.

Attaboy, Sterling.

Isaac drummed his fingers on the table. Autumn was fifteen minutes late, and he was getting antsy. Not only did he want to see her, but he didn't have much time.

Luckily, Devon and Deshauna were both at a friend's house for dinner, but they would be home soon and he wanted to be there before they arrived.

He sat back and toyed with his drink, a club soda for now, wondering if Autumn had received his email. She hadn't replied; nor had she spoken to him again all day, even though he was in his office, with the door open for most of it. Her door had remained closed, making him wish he had X-ray vision so he could see what she was doing.

He picked up his phone and shook his head at the irony.

Autumn was the first woman in a long time that he was interested in calling, yet he'd forgotten to get her personal cell number. That was a sure sign he'd lost his touch since becoming a father. But he had no regrets about adopting his children. He wanted to give them the life he never had growing up. He just hoped Devon and Deshauna would grow to love him as much as he loved them.

Isaac scrolled through photos of his kids and was so engrossed that he didn't see that Autumn had approached the table.

She cleared her throat and he quickly slid his phone back into his pocket. Perhaps one day he could tell her about his children, but not now.

He stood up, his fingers grazing her soft red sweater as he helped her out of her coat. She shivered, but he wasn't sure if it was from his touch or from the wintery bluster from which she'd just escaped.

A waiter approached to take their drink order.

"Is a bottle of red okay with you? It'll go great with that sweater."

Autumn's smile alone made her worth the wait.

She nodded and settled back in her chair. "So, I take it that the reason I'm here is because the meeting with Sterling did not go well."

Isaac blew out a breath. "No, it didn't. I think he would have thrown me out of his office if he could."

"Wow," Autumn said, shaking her head. "Has he always been uptight?"

"Yes, but it's never been this bad," he admitted. "But I bet having Felicia for a daughter doesn't help."

Autumn tried to stifle a giggle and failed. "That's mean. And I guess since it's only my second day at Paxton I shouldn't agree with you, but I think you might be right.

"I probably have no right to ask you this," Autumn said, tilting her head. "But is there anything going on with you and Felicia?"

Isaac almost choked on his wine. "No, nothing," he lied, now sorry he'd brought up her name in the conversation. Lately, he'd started to believe that Felicia was the one turning everyone against him at Paxton, including Sterling. He just didn't have any proof.

Autumn's eyes seemed to twinkle with some secret knowledge, and it made him nervous.

"Why, did she say something to you?"

She took a sip and shrugged. "Not particularly."

He set his wineglass on the table and decided that Autumn was just being coy.

Perhaps, instead of having information, she was digging for some. Maybe because she was interested in whether he was available or not. If she was, then it would be more difficult than ever to work with her. Feelings would start to develop on his part, and then what would he do? What could he do but break her heart?

There was only one way to find out. Maybe it was time to take a risk on more than the stock market. Maybe now was the time to take a risk on Autumn.

"You look beautiful tonight," he ventured.

One look at her face told Isaac she was not fooled. "Thank you, but you're changing the subject," she said drily. "Besides, I'm wearing the same thing I wore today."

"I know and I wanted to tell you earlier, but you had your door closed all day, for one."

"And the other?"

"The office wasn't the appropriate time or place."

She smiled and glanced around. "And this is?"

"Maybe," he replied nonchalantly. "It depends on how you feel about me."

She didn't speak for a while, only sipped her wine, and he began to feel like a fool for putting himself out there.

She set her wineglass down. "Listen, we should probably talk about the pitch, before we say or do things we really don't mean."

Now he really felt like a fool. He was thankful that she was acting as if she hadn't just dealt his ego a huge blow. It made it easier to shrug off her reaction as if he didn't care.

"Sure, but let's order some food first. I'm starved."

Autumn perused the menu. "I'm not really hungry, but I could go for some appetizers."

They ordered Thai scallops on a bed of mixed greens and fried tofu with homemade peach chutney.

Autumn opened up her bag and pulled out her tablet. "Let me share what I've learned so far. I've actually started a rough draft of the presentation."

He nodded his approval. "You're very proactive. That's one of the many things I like about you."

"Isaac. We're supposed to be talking about the pitch," she replied with the barest of smiles, and he could tell she was trying not to look pleased.

He grinned. "What? There's nothing in the Paxton handbook that says I can't compliment a coworker."

"I haven't read it so I'll have to trust you on that one." Autumn laughed. "Anyway, I took a look at the diamond market and I think it may be a good opportunity for Eleanor."

Isaac rubbed at his jaw. "Hmm. That's great, because when I suggested it, I was only kidding."

She put one hand on her hip. "*Now* you tell me?" she said, putting her hand on her hip. "I've spent hours researching."

He held up his hands. "Sorry, okay? Just let me know what you've found out."

Autumn docked the tablet and pulled up the presentation.

"Diamonds really have been the investor's best friend." She pointed to a graph. "They've outperformed equities since 2000. Plus, there are some new funds cropping up that could provide a way to invest without going direct to the wholesaler."

Isaac folded his arms across his chest and leaned forward. "Interesting. What else do you have?"

Autumn swiped her finger across the screen to advance to another slide. "Despite Eleanor's aversion to technology, I think investment in that sector is still a smart move. Plus, anything that involves green technology, such as hydroelectric engineering, is really hot right now."

The only hot thing he cared about was Autumn. But she made it clear for a second time that she wasn't interested.

Isaac leaned back in his chair. "This is a good start and we have a lot more work to do, but I like what I'm hearing. Go ahead and flesh out your recommendations. I'll need a complete analysis of each one, plus projections on how they'll perform over the next two, five and ten years."

He thought a moment. "I know a few people we can get in touch with to learn more about green technology, so you can put together a brief, but as for the diamond sector, you're on your own."

The food arrived, so Autumn powered off her tablet and stowed it in her bag.

"That's fine. I can do all that," she said, unfolding her napkin. "But I have one question."

"What's that?" he asked, licking his lips in anticipation of eating. Once he got some food into his stomach, maybe Autumn's rejection wouldn't hurt so much.

"How are you going to handle your attraction to me?"

Damn, but she was bold.

"I don't know. Take a cold shower twice a day." He shrugged, putting a forkful of scallops to his mouth.

He chewed and swallowed and paused. "Or maybe I'll just imagine you as a frog."

Autumn looked up from her plate and gasped. "Why a frog?"

"So I can kiss you and turn you into a princess."

She rolled her eyes, but he could see the smile she tried to hide, and he realized she enjoyed their ease at flirting as much as he did.

Isaac checked the time on his phone and reeled backward with surprise. It was getting late, if one considered six-thirty late, and he had missed a text from Deshauna that they would be home soon. He ran his hand over his head, worried that they'd get there before he did.

"Listen. Something's come up and I have to go."

He heard the tone of his voice and knew his excuse was lame, but it couldn't be helped.

Autumn put down her fork, her brow knit together with concern. "Is there anything wrong?"

"No, there's just somewhere I have to be soon." He reached for her hand and motioned to the waiter for the check. "I'm sorry to cut our evening short." He looked down at her still-full plate. "You barely got to eat."

Autumn pushed the food away. "It's okay. I've actually got somewhere I need to be, as well."

Now it was his turn to wonder if she was available or in a relationship, but he didn't dare ask.

He helped Autumn on with her coat and his fingers brushed her soft curls. He only had a short time left with her and he wanted to make the most of it. So he put a hundred dollar bill under his wineglass, knowing it would more than cover the check.

They made their way through the now-crowded restaurant to the entrance and saw that the snow had picked up considerably.

Isaac put his hand on Autumn's arm as she slipped on some gloves. "Where are you headed? It may be hard to get a cab now, especially in this weather. We can share one."

She finished wrapping her scarf around her neck and hesitated, as if she were considering the idea. "I'm going downtown, how about you?"

He shook his head, hoping the restaurant's dim lighting hid the disappointment in his eyes. "Uptown. Let's walk one block over to a side street—it may be easier to get a cab there."

She nodded in agreement and they both took deep breaths before Isaac opened the door.

The sidewalks were slick with ice and snow, but thankfully the wind was calm. Isaac immediately offered Autumn his arm to hold on to, but she refused and stuck her hands in her pockets. He wondered if she was upset about something. It was dark and snow was steadily falling, so it was hard to see her face.

A few yards later, she slipped rounding the corner. He grabbed on to her hand just in time, almost hitting the ground himself. This time when he tried to pull away, she didn't let go.

They were about halfway up the block when Isaac

spotted a place where they could wait for a cab without getting wetter than they already were.

He tightened his grip on Autumn's hand and pulled her into the alcove of The Rose Garden florist shop. A sign on the door read Closed Until Further Notice. He guessed the owners wouldn't mind if they loitered there awhile.

Isaac kept his back to the wall, positioning Autumn right in front of him to try to shield her from the cold as much as he could. He didn't need a thermometer to know that it was at or below freezing outside. Although they'd only been outside a few minutes, their coats and hair already had a light dusting of snow.

"I've got a perfect view of the street here, so I can watch for a cab and keep you out of this nasty weather."

"Thanks," she said in a jittery voice. "I'm freezing."

She started to shake her head side to side, but he reached out and cupped her face in his hands.

"Don't do that," he said. "All those snowflakes caught in your curls make you look like a princess."

She lifted her chin, the tiny droplets of melting snow on her face seemed to glisten.

"How can this frog be a princess when she's never been kissed?"

That was all Isaac needed to hear.

He sucked in a breath, not giving his mind time to think or to worry or to even care about tomorrow.

"I can take care of that right now," he whispered.

He closed his eyes and slowly guided her face to his, relying on sense rather than sight to that first taste he knew he would never forget.

And Autumn did not disappoint. Her lips were soft and warm and surprisingly insistent upon his, and in the haze of their kisses, he felt her fingers on his chest, unbuttoning his coat. The shocking blast of cold made him lift his lips from hers. He gasped aloud, but it was quickly silenced by the mellow warmth of her body against his chest. He bit his lip, going rock hard as she snuggled against him.

His back muscles tensed under her roaming hands, the pleasure of her touch unfamiliar, and her fingers kneaded his flesh as if seeking answers. They stumbled against the alcove wall and he wove his hands in her hair, their breath intermingling in the cold air, eyes transfixed on each other. In their gaze, a message of truth. They knew what they both wanted, but there wasn't much time.

Then his tongue met flesh again, seared the inside of her mouth, and their lips moved together. They kissed and kissed, not devouring but savoring like a fine wine, not wanting it to end. This moment was as fragile as the snowflakes that swirled around them.

He felt her breasts rub against his chest, flaring his passions, and he yearned to touch them, but he didn't want to open her coat and have her get cold.

Angling his hands under her coat and beneath her skirt, he molded his hands around her buttocks. His tongue licked the corners of her mouth almost delicately before taking a surprise plunge into her mouth. At the same time, he cupped her round behind, lifting her up and securing her firmly against him.

With a low moan into his mouth, she wrapped her

legs around his waist and his fingers sank into her soft flesh. Her heat fanned invitingly against his trousers; his constrained penis thumped in the hopes that she'd let him in.

The sound of her panty hose ripping pushed him over the edge and he broke the kiss. Staring into her eyes, his torso involuntarily started to slowly pulse against her and into that coven of heat, as if there were no fabric there at all.

His pace steadily increased and she tightened her grip around his waist and found his lips again, an anchor point on which to suck and hold. With every hard and desperate grind of their bodies, she held on.

Oh, how she held on.

Isaac threw his head back against the wall, nearly losing his senses of time and place when out of the corner of his eye he saw a cab ambling down the road.

"Damn," he muttered, releasing her.

He ran out to the curb, almost slipping on the ice, lifted his right hand and waved.

"Taxi!" he shouted, breathing heavy, the flaps of his coat wide open.

He didn't know whether to be happy or mad when the cabbie pulled over.

Isaac turned just in time to see Autumn smooth her hand over her coat. She picked up her tote bag and gingerly stepped onto the sidewalk. When she reached the cab, her breathing was steady.

"Are you okay?" he asked, touching her arm.

Autumn nodded but didn't meet his eyes as he opened the door and she stepped into the taxi. A moment later, she was gone. As he trudged up the road to the subway, Isaac's heart squeezed in his chest, wondering how he was going to face her in the morning.

Chapter 6

Autumn scowled at the stack of files on her desk. She hadn't wanted to lug them to the restaurant last night, possibly inviting questions from Isaac, so she had double the number to go through today.

Thank God, it was Friday. She couldn't wait to go home, open up a bottle of wine and not think about paperwork or the Paxton investigation for a while.

But she knew she wouldn't be able to forget about last night.

She rose and closed the blinds against the sunlight streaming through the windows. When she turned, she saw that Isaac's door was still closed, his office dark. It was after ten in the morning.

The doorman hadn't called this morning, and when

she inquired why, he told her that Isaac hadn't gone out for his run, so there was no reason to contact her.

She almost asked him to go up and check on him, to see if he was there, but she didn't want the man to be more suspicious than he probably was. Free money only worked for a while. Eventually he would start to ask her questions or, worse, tell Isaac that she was spying on him.

Autumn sat back at her desk and wrung her hands.

Where was he? She couldn't help feeling something bad had happened to him.

She felt a pang of guilt remembering how he'd allowed her to take the first taxi. It was a sweet, chivalrous gesture, because she knew he had somewhere else to go, someone else waiting for him to arrive. When she looked back, he had already turned and was walking away, and there were no more cabs coming down the street.

Had he even made it home last night?

Calm down, she told herself. There must be a logical explanation for his absence. Perhaps he had a morning meeting with a client. She only hoped he wasn't avoiding her, because she needed to talk to him about last night.

In the heat of the moment, they'd both forgotten about the real purpose of working together, which was to insure Eleanor Witterman became Paxton's newest client.

And of course, while Isaac was kissing her senseless, the last thing on her mind was the investigation.

Sterling wouldn't be too happy if he knew either. In fact, he'd probably fire both of them.

Autumn twisted a curl around her finger.

"That can't happen," she said aloud.

Felicia suddenly appeared in the doorway. "What can't happen?" She stepped into the room and glanced around. "Who are you talking to?"

Autumn's stomach clenched. "Myself. Haven't you ever done that?"

"What? Talked to myself?" Felicia shook her head. "People might think I'm crazy."

"Not if you're telling the truth," Autumn replied.

Felicia's eyes narrowed. "Exactly what are you implying?"

"Nothing," Autumn replied. "I'm only saying that talking to yourself doesn't mean you're crazy."

Felicia looked Autumn up and down. "Humph," she snapped. "That's your opinion."

If Autumn wasn't the confident woman that she was, she might have felt like an ant under Felicia's scrutiny. However, she knew that the woman had something to hide and she was determined to get past her obnoxious attitude to the facts.

Autumn folded her hands on her desk. "How can I help you? I'm sure you didn't stop by my office for idle chitchat."

"Good. You are starting to get to know me and how I work. I do have a purpose for being here."

Felicia dropped her hands, slowly sat down and crossed her legs, like a beauty-pageant wannabe practicing how to be graceful.

"I understand you are working with Isaac on the Witterman pitch."

"That's correct. In fact, we had a dinner meeting last night to talk strategy."

Felicia's eyes darkened suspiciously. "Why dinner? You couldn't meet here at the office?"

"No, Isaac was in meetings all day and that was the only time he could get together."

"Well!" she exclaimed. "Sounds like someone needs a seminar on time management!"

"I'd love one, but I don't have time for it," Autumn replied with a giggle.

But Felicia wasn't smiling and Autumn's face burned with embarrassment.

She cleared her throat. "So what about the project?"

Felicia moved her chair closer to the desk. "I want you to keep a very close eye on Isaac," she revealed. Her voice dropped down to almost a whisper. "There has been some talk among the employees and something isn't right."

Autumn held back a laugh. She couldn't believe her ears. Felicia actually wanted her to spy on Isaac.

"But you're the director of human resources. Why not just come out and ask him yourself?"

"Because he reports to my father, that's why, who adores him and thinks the world of him. He'd be really upset if I did anything like that."

"I see. Well, I'm not sure if I'm comfortable with this. I mean, I just started at Paxton. What possible repercussions can I expect to my career here?"

Felicia sat back, her eyes widening. "Why, absolutely

none at all," she insisted, sounding appalled at the question. "You have nothing to worry about. All you need to do is watch for anything improper that you find that could hurt the company, and report it to me first, not my father."

Autumn hesitated. Had Sterling told Felicia that she was really a private investigator? Was that what this was all about?

"I don't know about this. I'm an analyst, not a private eye."

Felicia exhaled impatiently. "I know that, Autumn. That's why you're perfect. You can actually discover any wrongdoing."

Autumn blew out a breath, inwardly relieved that her cover seemed to be still intact. "And you expect me to go behind your father's back with any information and come straight to you."

Felicia nodded. "Maybe you won't find anything. But if you do, I want to know about it first."

She pointed her finger at Autumn. "One more thing. If you try to hide anything you find out, you'll get a chance to see firsthand just how brutal life at Paxton can really be."

When Felicia left, Autumn wanted to laugh at her attempt to frighten her, but instead she threaded her hands through her curls. Now she was working for Sterling and Felicia against Isaac, and neither of them knew about the other.

Isaac clutched the paper bag that held his deli sandwich and a bag of salt-and-vinegar chips that he always ate when he was having a particularly stressful day and strode into the Paxton Building.

It was nearly one o'clock and his stomach was grumbling as if it hadn't had food to churn in weeks. After a morning chock-full of off-site meetings, all he wanted to do was eat and catch up on email.

Riding up in the elevator, a part of him hoped Autumn was still at lunch. Isaac didn't want to avoid her, not that he could anyway. Quite the contrary. He just needed more time to figure out how to handle what could turn out to be an uncomfortable situation.

If she wanted an explanation of why he kissed her, he couldn't give her one. If she wanted an apology, he couldn't give her that either. He sure as hell wasn't sorry he kissed her. He was only sorry that their kiss had to end so abruptly.

On the executive floor, he walked down the hallway to his office a little slower than usual and then, deciding he was acting silly, resumed his normal pace.

Autumn's door was open, but from his vantage point he couldn't tell if she was there. But he knew that she could see him through the little glass window. That's how Felicia had spied on him, before she'd tried to seduce him just weeks earlier.

Isaac clenched his jaw in disgust at the memory. How long had Felicia been watching him?

He dug his key out of his pocket and took a deep breath to relax, thankful that the room where Felicia had tried to destroy him was now occupied by a woman from which he welcomed seduction.

"Hey, stranger," she called out. "Are you okay?"

Isaac's heart leaped in surprise. Instead of being upset, her cheerful voice sounded like she was glad he was there.

"Yeah," he grunted, fumbling with the keys. "Give me a second to unload this stuff."

Opening the door, he flipped on the light, hung up his coat and carefully put his lunch and laptop bag on his desk. Then he walked into Autumn's office, hesitating only a moment before shutting the door. Whatever was about to transpire between them, he didn't want anyone to hear or see. As far as anyone knew, they were simply discussing business.

Isaac pulled out the chair in front of her desk and sat down. His eyes traced her lips as she wiped her mouth.

"Tough morning?" she asked, replacing the plastic top over a container of half-eaten salad.

"Tough clients," he said and sighed, stretching his legs out in front of him. "I think investment banking is the only business in the world where the customer isn't always right, but that doesn't make telling them when they're wrong any easier."

Autumn poked a straw into a bottle of mineral water and nodded. "But all is forgiven when the money starts rolling in, right?"

He shrugged. "So far I've been lucky."

Autumn stood and walked around the desk. She tossed the salad container into the trash and he watched as she slowly walked around the desk. Her pale pink suit wasn't skintight but was perfectly tailored to complement her hourglass shape.

She sat down opposite him. "What's the secret to your success?" she asked, crossing her legs.

For a split second, Isaac imagined her legs wide open, and only for him. He swallowed hard to rid his mind of the fantasy, knowing that she could only belong to him in his dreams.

"Intuition, I guess."

Her eyebrows knit together. "What do you mean?"

He settled back deeper in his chair, trying to put some imaginary distance between them. "Knowing when to push and knowing when to pull back."

Autumn exhaled. "Ah. Like when you kissed me." Her eyes flitted briefly to the door and back to him. "Somehow you knew I wanted you, too."

Her confession of lust baffled his mind, but his flesh knew exactly how to respond. He shifted in his seat and said nothing, wondering if she was trying to trick him.

He'd been burned once before in this very office.

Never again.

At his silence, she pursed her lips. "Didn't you?"

Her tone was so playful and teasing that he realized he wanted to explore the meaning behind her words almost as much as he wanted to explore her.

"I didn't know," he replied, shaking his head. "I took a chance."

Isaac dipped his eyes to the single pearl nestled at the base of her neck. Her modest blouse revealed nothing but the memory of her breasts against his body.

"I didn't want to stop. Is that wrong?"

She closed her eyes briefly. "No, but that taxi came along at just the right time."

He reached for her hand. "I wish it hadn't."

Gently, he lifted her hand to his mouth, bent his head and moved his lips across her knuckles.

She whooshed in a breath and her eyes flapped open. "Th-that taxi probably saved our careers."

Autumn pulled her hand out of his light grasp. She laughed nervously.

"Or at least mine," she continued. "I mean, what would people think? I've been here barely a week and I— They'll think I'm trying to make a play for you when all I wanted was—"

"To be kissed," Isaac cut in, realizing that what he thought was a deep attraction to him was nothing more than a spur-of-the-moment mistake.

She folded her hands in her lap as if to dissuade him from touching her. "You know when you haven't done something in a while and all of a sudden you get the opportunity?"

Her eyes danced with excitement, but not for him.

"Sure, when you're with someone you feel in your heart is safe, you just go for it," he replied.

Was that why he felt so comfortable with Autumn, because something about her felt safe to him?

Autumn blew out a breath. "I knew you'd understand. From what I've read about you, you're at the top of your career."

She stood, her pelvis close enough to reach. Close enough for him to pull up that skirt she was neatly smoothing and allow his hands—and his mouth—to mess it up again.

"You wouldn't risk it all for an office romance."

Oh, wouldn't I?

He rose carefully, hating that his flesh didn't get the memo that Autumn was off-limits. Still, he didn't bother to conceal the bulge in his pants. Let her see, and then imagine, what she was missing.

Isaac pushed the chair back with his heel, to allow plenty of space between them.

"You're right, Autumn. Why take a risk when you already know it will fail?"

Her head jerked back as if his words stung something deep inside her. Rather than ask if he'd hurt her, he simply headed to the door, not wanting to hear the answer.

Isaac turned back to see that she hadn't moved from where she'd been standing.

"But hey," he retorted, knowing he was trying to sound a lot more macho than he felt at the moment. "If you ever want to be kissed again, you know where I am."

He walked out hoping she'd take a risk and knowing, for both of their sakes, that she probably wouldn't.

Chapter 7

When Autumn left work that afternoon, Isaac's door was closed. She had no idea if he was in there or not, and she certainly wasn't going to knock. Not that he wanted to talk to her anyway.

After she'd rejected him earlier, Autumn realized she had two choices: solve the case or fall in love. She was being paid to find answers, not hop into bed with Isaac. Although the prospect of hot sex with one of NYC's wealthiest men was beyond thrilling, she had a feeling one night with him would never be enough.

A relationship, even a brief one, wouldn't be fair to either of them. Besides, she was far too much of a free spirit to be tied down, and she never knew where or when her next case would come along. There was something about digging into people's lives to find the truth that eased her loneliness.

Most of the time.

Once outside the Paxton Building, she adjusted her tote bag, heavy with files she needed to review over the weekend. The sooner she discovered something wrong, some kind of misdoing to pin on Isaac, the better. But so far, the only thing he was guilty of was turning her on.

The subway uptown, always unbearable, was even worse on a Friday afternoon, with everyone jostling to get wherever they were going. Her nerves were frazzled and her back ached, but not as much as her heart. She couldn't wait to get home, relax and try to forget about Isaac.

Autumn moved with the flow of humanity up the stairs onto Columbus Circle. Upon arriving at her apartment, she wanted to scream in frustration. One of the elevators was out of order and the other one was already filled to capacity with residents.

Not including the penthouse levels, there were over fifty floors in her building. Autumn adjusted her bag, leaned against the mirrored wall and groaned. It looked like she was going to be waiting awhile.

A few minutes later, two kids approached the elevators. One was a teenage girl who wore a smirk instead of a smile. The other was a boy who lagged slightly behind carrying two grocery bags. Autumn could tell by the strained look on his face that they were too heavy for him. Both children wore school uniforms and pricey designer coats, not with haughty confidence but as though their bodies didn't belong in them.

The boy frowned. "What's wrong with the elevator?"

"Can't you read, stupid?" The girl scowled, pointing the sign. "It says it's out of order."

"Signs can't talk," he retorted. "So who's the real dummy?"

The two started arguing and the decibels started elevating and Autumn wished she knew how to whistle through her fingers to get them to stop. But she didn't. Nor did she have any experience with children. However, she did watch reruns of *The Facts of Life.*

Autumn held up her hands as if she was directing traffic.

"Children, children," she intoned in her best impression of a housemother's voice. "Now if you will just quiet down, the elevator will be here shortly, and we can all go home."

Even though she left out the milk-and-cookies part, which she knew was the standard bribe, they shut their mouths and stared at her.

"I know another way up," the boy blurted out, looking over his shoulder. "The doorman is busy. Let's go."

He was either really convincing or Autumn was just tired of waiting, but she followed them around the corner and down a couple of hallways that she'd never seen before, until they stopped at an elevator she never knew existed.

"What's this? And yes, before you get smart, I know it's an elevator."

"It's for the penthouse apartments only," he explained. "We never use it. Our dad won't let us. He makes us ride in the regular elevators with everyone else."

His sister clucked her teeth. "That's because we are like everyone else."

"No, we're not. Not anymore," he insisted. "We're rich!"

Autumn blew out a breath. "Congratulations," she interjected, not wanting to get in the middle of another argument. "Now, if you guys will excuse me, I don't live in a penthouse, so I think I'll just go back and see if the regular elevators are working."

She turned to leave and she heard the rustling of plastic.

"Wait," the boy called out, looping both bags through one hand. "Why don't you come up with us? My sister is making dinner for my dad tonight. He can't cook and sometimes we get tired of ordering takeout."

The girl rolled her eyes at her brother. "What would Dad say if you invited a perfect stranger into his home?"

"It's our home now, too," the boy corrected. "And I think he'd thank us."

Autumn raised an eyebrow, intrigued. "Why's that?"

"Because you're really cute, and he's really lonely."

She smiled at the sincerity in the boy's voice. He seemed so eager to please, while his sister seemed the total opposite.

"Stop crushing on her," she ordered, obviously trying to embarrass him. "Dad doesn't need you to play matchmaker."

"Why not?" he objected. "I'm a lot safer than a dating website and I don't require a password."

Autumn burst out laughing. "Thank you for the invitation, but I really must be going."

The boy shrugged and pressed the elevator button. "Okay. But if you change your mind, my name is Devon and this is my sister, Deshauna. What's your name?"

"I'm Autumn. Pleased to meet you."

For once she was glad her hands were full, so she wouldn't have to shake hands. Children were walking playgrounds for germs and she didn't have the time to get sick right now. As if she ever did.

The elevator doors opened and the kids got in.

"Good luck with dinner and thanks again," Autumn said patiently. By the time she finally got up to her apartment, she'd need two glasses of wine instead of one.

The doors began to close. "He's a nice guy," Devon called out. "And his name is Isaac."

Autumn's heart took a nosedive and she stared at the elevator in shock.

And my cover is blown.

Isaac rolled down the window and leaned his head against the taxi's backseat. He could have taken the subway but just didn't want to deal with the hassle tonight. At least here he could be alone and have a chance to think before going home and dealing with whatever challenges his children had faced that day.

The icy air hit his nostrils as the cab sped down the street. He breathed in deeply, trying to clear his mind of the woman who had so easily lit a fire within his heart and—just as easily—doused it that very afternoon. No woman he'd actively pursued had ever rejected him before. Why had she?

Turning his head, he stared out of the window at the shops rolling by as they traveled down Fifth Avenue. The fancy storefronts, all lit up and glittering like diamonds, were filled with things most people couldn't afford. They say money can't buy love, but he sure as hell would pay just about anything to be with Autumn.

It hardly mattered anymore. All he had to do was get through the Witterman pitch and he wouldn't have to work with her again. She'd move down to the floor where all the other analysts were and he would rarely see her. The constant temptation to kiss her, to touch her, would hopefully go away. Still, if the ache in his chest and the bulge in his pants were any indication, he was starting to get the feeling that there was nothing as painful as letting something go before it even had a chance to begin.

When he arrived at his apartment building, he paid the cab fare and greeted the doorman, instructing him to have his dry cleaning picked up early the following morning.

As he rode the private elevator to his penthouse, his heart was heavy with regret for even thinking that he could have any kind of relationship with Autumn. When the doors opened, he palmed the lower half of his face in exasperation. For the first time ever, he'd actually forgotten to bring home dinner!

"Hey, guys, where do you want to go to eat tonight?" he called out.

He set his laptop bag down on the marble floor and

wrinkled his nose at the scent of steak wafting through the air. And it didn't smell burned.

"Surprise!" his children shouted as he walked into the kitchen.

Isaac was astonished at the sight of the round glass table, beautifully set for three with the china plates he'd bought years earlier thinking someday he'd use them, plus real, not plastic silverware. In the middle, a giant pitcher of lemonade with the actual lemons floating in it was surrounded by little votive candles.

He turned his attention to his two children. "What is this?"

"We made dinner," Devon said. "Steak and mashed potatoes with gravy. A real man's meal."

Deshauna rolled her eyes and nodded. "Yeah. Having takeout all the time gets old. So we decided to change things up a little bit." She bit her lip and then said, almost shyly, "Is it okay that we did all this?"

Isaac's heart melted and he moved to wrap them in a hug. "It's more than okay," he assured. "It's fantastic."

Ever since adopting Devon and Deshauna, he worried constantly that he wasn't doing enough. Being enough.

But maybe he was. Maybe the knowledge that he was there with them and for them forever was finally sinking in. Isaac wasn't going away or abandoning them. Maybe that was all his children needed to finally realize that he loved them.

They were no longer foster—they were family.

He hugged them tighter. "I know I'm new at this father thing, and that one of those cooking shows would never hire me, but I'm so happy you guys are mine."

"We are too, Dad," Devon said, his voice muffled against Isaac's shoulder. "But I've got to get the steaks now."

"And you're ruining my hair!" Deshauna shrieked.

"Okay. Okay," Isaac acquiesced, releasing them. "But be forewarned, if the meal is real good, I just might want to read you two a bedtime story."

Devon and Deshauna groaned and then got busy putting the food on the table while Isaac sat down. When everything was ready, he bowed his head and said grace, thanking God for his wonderful children. In his mind, he asked for strength where Autumn was concerned, grateful that thoughts of her were put on hold for now.

Isaac cut into his steak and took a bite. It was surprisingly flavorful. The mashed potatoes were light and fluffy, and the gravy had just enough of a savory kick that he poured even more on his plate.

"This is awesome. I guess all those hours watching food shows finally paid off!"

"I have another surprise for you, Dad," Devon said through a mouthful of food. "We found you a girl to date!"

Isaac stopped chewing. "Who?"

Devon slurped his lemonade and set his glass down. "Her name is Autumn and she's really hot."

"Gross," Deshauna huffed in disgust. They started to bicker back and forth, but Isaac barely heard a word.

Devon couldn't be talking about *his* Autumn. Could he?

"Oh, really?" Isaac put down his fork and peered at

his son. "And where did you meet this gorgeous creature?"

"Right here in our building. She lives here. Isn't that perfect?"

Yes. Perfect.

He cleared his throat, trying to buy time as both children looked at him expectantly. He had to play this right. Since he'd become a father, there hadn't been a woman in his life. Yes, he wanted one. He wanted Autumn. But he had to play this right.

"What did she say when you told her about me?"

"She didn't say anything," Deshauna piped up. "She just ran."

Isaac raised an eyebrow. Surely his daughter was exaggerating. "She ran?"

"Well, not exactly, but Devon invited her to dinner and she said no," Deshauna explained. "Then she ran."

"She had pretty hair, Dad. It was all curly."

"Her hair was all right," Deshauna stated with a hint of jealousy. "It looked frizzy to me."

"It sounds like she wasn't interested, kids. Thanks anyway. But you know there's a lesson in all this. If someone runs away from you, you should run, too."

Too bad he wasn't going to follow his own advice.

Instead, he was going to follow his heart.

Later that evening after Devon and Deshauna were in bed, Isaac took a long, hot shower. Afterward he pulled on a white T-shirt and a pair of comfortable sweats and slid into his well-worn leather slippers.

He took the private elevator downstairs to the lobby

and spoke to the doorman. After giving the man a large tip, he got on the regular elevator up to the forty-eighth floor. He only hesitated a second before knocking on the door of apartment 3G.

Autumn opened the door and nearly took his breath away. She was clad in an ivory robe that only accentuated her already-gorgeous skin tone. He could see a hint of pale yellow lace as she crossed her arms over her chest.

"Isaac!"

She actually seemed surprised to see him.

He leaned against the doorway. "You opened that door pretty quickly. I hope you looked through the peephole. We do live in New York and you never know what kind of crazy could be lurking in the hallways."

Her hair was bunched up into some kind of messy bun. She tucked an errant strand behind her ear. "Of course I did," she retorted, sounding irritated. "What are you doing here?"

"I live in this building. Why didn't you tell me you did, too?" he demanded, his voice echoing in the hallway. He knew he was being loud, but he couldn't help it. He was angry.

Autumn placed a finger to her lips. "Shh…do you know what time it is?"

"Yeah. It's way past time for you to tell me the truth, and I'm not leaving until you do."

Autumn stared at him a moment and then stepped aside. "Come in. But you can't stay long."

She closed the door, locked it and put her hands on

her hips. "What makes you think I knew you lived in the same building as me?"

Isaac opened his mouth to speak but then shut it to ponder her very logical question. He knew she had a good point. It was almost as if he was accusing her of lying to him, of hiding something. But why would she do that?

"Let me guess," Autumn continued quickly. "Your ego is so big that you thought I moved in here to try to meet the wealthiest bachelor in New York City. You probably think that's why I wanted to work at Paxton, to get close to you. Didn't you?"

"No. I—I thought..." He ran a hand over his head, feeling like a fool. "Listen, Autumn. I don't know what I was thinking."

When Autumn furrowed her brow and looked at him like he was crazy, suddenly he knew the reason he was acting like a paranoid fool.

"Ever since Felicia, I—" he blurted.

"Felicia?" Autumn interrupted. "What does she have to do with this?"

Isaac cursed inwardly for even saying that woman's name out loud. Even though he'd made it clear that he wasn't interested in her, she was still causing trouble for him. She was like a curse.

"I think we better talk," she acknowledged, gesturing toward the living room. "Please have a seat."

Although Isaac was sure nothing good could come from talking about Felicia, he nodded and followed her across the room.

As Autumn cleared stuff from the couch, he admired

the way her robe cleaved to her hips and draped over her round bottom.

She stacked a bunch of files on the floor next to her, sat down and crossed her legs.

Isaac sat down carefully as he was starting to get a little aroused at the sight of her bare feet. Her toenails were painted a light pink and were almost begging to be sucked.

He stared at her, almost not believing he was in the same room with her. It was so different from seeing her in the office. He liked it. The playing field was leveled.

Here he was just a man. And she was just a woman.

A woman he wanted to know and to savor, and maybe…to love.

She narrowed her eyes at him. "You're staring at me. What did I do now?"

He exhaled and shook his head. "Nothing. It's just that you're even more beautiful at eleven at night than you are at eleven in the morning."

She put her hands on her hips. "Are you saying I look bad in the morning?" she huffed, not noticing that her robe had fallen open just enough to reveal the lush curves hidden beneath lace.

"No!" Isaac reached for her hand. "I'm saying I could look at you twenty-four hours a day. Is that wrong?"

She ignored his hand and instead pulled her robe closed again so roughly that a few tendrils of hair escaped from her bun and skimmed her shoulders.

"You don't have to flatter me, Isaac."

"I can if it's true and if it will bring a smile back to your face," he said warmly.

"I'm sorry." She closed her eyes briefly, then opened them and scanned the room. "You caught me at a bad time and this place is a mess."

"Working on a Friday night? Even I don't do that!" he teased, pointing at the stack of paperwork on the floor.

"Have you looked at a calendar lately, Isaac? The Witterman pitch is a week from today. I thought it best to keep the momentum going on it."

Isaac knew the timeline was closing in on them, which was part of the reason he was glad Autumn lived in the same building. It would make working on the project all the easier, plus the added bonus that he could be alone with Autumn without anyone knowing.

The other reason was that he had to convince her to keep his children a secret.

"I'm sure Sterling would appreciate all your effort if he knew," Isaac said.

"Well, I don't plan on telling him. I don't think he's interested in the mechanics of how it's put together. All he cares about is the end result, and that's what I'm going to deliver."

Isaac leaned back against the cushions. "You're going to deliver?" he said, aghast. "Aren't I part of this team?"

Autumn pursed her lips. "Of course. I didn't mean to offend you." She glanced down at her lap. "But after our conversation this morning, I just thought—"

"That I didn't want to work with you because you rejected me?" he offered.

She looked up and nodded, and Isaac could tell she was embarrassed.

"And I thought you didn't want to work with me." Isaac smiled. "I guess we were both wrong."

Autumn smiled back. "You mentioned Felicia earlier. Where does she fit in all this?"

"She tried to seduce me a couple of months ago and I wasn't buying it. Besides, she's Sterling's daughter. If I were to get involved with her, I might as well kiss my career goodbye."

He sighed. "Anyway, ever since that happened, I feel that she's out to get me."

"I see. And do you have any proof of that?"

"No, not yet, but if she found out I have children, I know she would tell Sterling, and he would not be happy. He's not exactly pro-family. He feels that work should come first, no matter what."

"What made you decide to adopt?"

Isaac paused and heaved a deep sigh. Under Autumn's inquisitive gaze, it wasn't easy to hide. So he decided to take a risk.

"I grew up in a foster home. I know what it's like to be a slave to the system that is supposed to help you. I have money. I have a nice home and I sure have enough love to give. When I met Devon and Deshauna, I knew they needed me, and quite frankly, I needed them, too. I can't let anything break us apart."

Isaac flattened his palms together and realized they were slightly clammy. Embarrassed, he rubbed his hands together until they were dry, rather than wipe them on his clothes.

Autumn smiled and seemed not to notice his discomfort. "That's a wonderful story. And it sounds like everything worked out."

"It has so far, but sometimes I get a strange feeling that things are about to change."

Autumn shook her head. "Is that why you haven't told anyone?"

He nodded. "Yeah. Besides the fact that it's just wrong to keep them a secret, I'm supposed to claim them for health insurance purposes. But I'm afraid that if Sterling finds out that I have other priorities besides making money for Paxton, I could lose my job and my chance at making partner."

"That would never happen. You're the most successful investment banker he has on staff."

"Oh no? He and I haven't exactly been on good terms lately. It wouldn't be hard for him to pluck a new graduate from Harvard Business School and groom him, like he did me, twelve years ago."

Isaac inched his body closer and reached for her hand again. "If I promise not to flatter you anymore, can you promise me that you won't tell my secret?"

She looked down at his hand briefly and laughed. "What if I like it when you flatter me?"

"Then I will just have to find some other way to convince you to keep my secret."

Autumn lifted her eyes and tilted her head. "Sounds intriguing."

The seductive lilt in her voice put him at ease. He leaped from the couch and pulled her up with him.

She giggled a little. "What's going on?"

"Come with me. I want to show you something."

Isaac held her hand and walked over to the floor-to-ceiling window that spanned the length of the living room.

"Now look outside," he commanded. "We're forty-eight stories up. What do you see?"

"Central Park West," Autumn responded, confusion in her eyes. "What's this all about, Isaac?"

He applied gentle pressure on Autumn's shoulders to turn her toward the window again. Wrapping his arms around her waist, he pulled her close to him until her soft buttocks connected with his torso. When they rolled against the hard ridge of flesh beneath his sweatpants, he bit his lip to stop from groaning.

He traced his lips along one ear and she trembled in his arms. "You want to know what I see?"

At her nod, Isaac placed his cheek next to hers.

"I see a city with a million secrets."

He moved his lips along the velvety-smooth skin of her jawline. "What's one more?"

She hitched in a breath as Isaac quickly untied the belt of her robe and slid it from her shoulders. The light swoosh as the garment fell to the floor was the only sound in the room.

Isaac grew even harder at the sight of the thin ribbon of lace covering her otherwise bare shoulders and the deep vee of skin on her back.

She was still facing the window as he kicked off his shoes and clasped his hands around her waist. At night, he wore no underwear under his cotton sweats so there was no mistaking his physical excitement, both by feel and by sight. When she wriggled her bottom against him suggestively and gasped, he knew she felt his need for her.

He pulled her even closer to him and now he freely groaned aloud, fighting the urge to bend her at the waist and make her his, right now. He wanted to go slow, but she had made him so hard.

Struggling to maintain control, Isaac decided he would explore her by touch first. He flattened his palms on her abdomen. It was taut and flat, just the way he liked it. He spread his long fingers wide until both hands nearly covered her middle.

As he scaled his hands down even lower, she moaned deeply, the vibrations rolling from her body to his, and his fingertips stopped their journey a few inches below her belly button.

Isaac patted the small mound of hair that tantalized him beneath her nightgown. The treasure of this woman would be his and his alone.

"Are you wet for me yet, baby?"

With a nod, Autumn whimpered and he reversed his movements, denying both of them. Slowly he trailed his hands skyward along her body until they enclosed her breasts, still trapped beneath the silky fabric. He didn't even have to look at them to know they were beautiful, because they felt beautiful, so large and full in his palms, complete with nipples as hard as pegs.

Isaac licked his lips at his discovery and circled each tip with the pad of his thumb, breathing hard as the surrounding areola puckered immediately at his light touch.

"Oh," Autumn cried out. She raised her arms above

her head and looped them around his neck, giving him easier access.

He bent his head and planted featherlight kisses down her neck as he massaged her breasts until she arched her back away from him and thrust her nipples into the air.

Still standing behind her, Isaac lifted her nightgown to her waist. He slid the index finger of his left hand down the cleft of her buttocks and then, reaching around her waist, he slid the fingers of his right hand between her legs. She was slick and hot and ready.

My God, he thought, thumping his penis gently against her soft ass, she's so wet, so wet.

She dropped her arms from his neck and moaned, and he used that opportunity to remove the nightgown. Tossing it behind him, he moved in front of her, watching her eyes move down his body and widen at the sight of his penis tenting forth in his pants.

Autumn, her eyes glowing in the dim light, was now naked before him, and his mouth watered at the sight of her luscious body and all the curves and the shadows and the secret places he'd yet to explore.

The fact that they stood before windows that spanned the entire length of the room added to the excitement of the moment for both of them.

Autumn reached for him, touching the tip of his flesh jutting under his sweats, and that was enough for him to cave.

Isaac pulled her into his arms and kissed her deeply, and his heart pounded when her tongue slipped into his mouth first. He allowed her to take the lead for a while as she threaded her hands through his hair and kissed him with a fervor that left him gasping for breath.

When he broke away, her eyes were ablaze with the kind of heat that he knew he would always strive to attain.

Grasping her by the waist with both hands, Isaac bent his head to her breast. He flicked his tongue at one nipple, bouncing the stiff peak between his lips before launching into a full-on suck that had Autumn thrashing about in his arms.

She held on to his head as he traced his hands from her waist to her ass. He held on, wedging his mouth and tongue underneath her heavy breasts, before planting a soft kiss on her navel. Moving his hands to her slick inner thighs, which were quivering from his touch, he knew it was time.

Isaac sank to his knees on the carpet and buried his face in the heat of Autumn's wiry curls, inhaling her earthy scent. Carefully, he spread her moist outer lips with his fingers until he exposed the sensitive core of her desire.

Licking slowly, his tongue discovered every juicy curve and fleshy mound, while she writhed and moaned and at times cried out, bending and succumbing to the most secret of pleasures.

And at that moment, neither cared about the aftermath of their passion. It was hidden in the subtle glow of streetlights, the seedy darkness of alleyways, the pulsing music of an after-hours club and the tangled sheets of a lover's bed.

Chapter 8

Autumn awoke the next morning so drowsy she couldn't even remember how she'd got into bed. Then her thighs began to tingle and the memories came flooding back. Erotic ones that made her burrow under her covers and wish the pleasure never had to end.

Isaac.

What that man could do with his lips, his tongue and his mouth should be illegal.

Even though she was a private investigator, after last night, she'd break every law in the book to feel that way again.

She yawned, and the fantasy was broken as she realized how close she'd come last night to revealing the truth about herself.

When she'd met his kids, she was sure her cover

was blown and that Isaac would somehow know why she was really at Paxton. But as soon as he appeared at her apartment, she knew that, logically, there was no way he could know. Her assumption had been the result of panic.

Thank goodness she'd realized that in time; otherwise, she might not have had the fortune of a night she knew she'd never forget.

It was clear that he wanted her and that she wanted him. But even after she'd decided to play along in their game of desire, she hadn't expected Isaac to take himself out of the equation and focus completely on her needs.

Her body still thrummed from his gift, orgasm upon orgasm, until she thought she'd go mad. No man had ever done that before so willingly, so expertly. And yet, she knew her satisfaction would not be complete until she was one with him.

But that hadn't happened. When she'd collapsed in his arms, shaking and nearly incoherent, Isaac had carried her into her bedroom and held her until she fell asleep. Why hadn't he made love to her then, when he had ample opportunity? She found it noble that he refused to take advantage of her, and yet it raised her suspicions, too.

She stretched and the covers fell away. Her skin had goose pimples in the cool air and she rubbed her bare shoulders, having forgotten to set the thermostat to her normal bedtime temperature. Just as she'd forgotten that she was supposed to be working on busting Isaac.

She sat up and threaded her fingers through her hair,

recalling Felicia's request that she keep an eye on Isaac, drawing further suspicion that he'd done something wrong.

Now she understood why Isaac was concerned Felicia would find out about his children. Turns out he was right to worry. The woman obviously didn't take rejection well.

It was clear to her that Felicia's request would ultimately lead to revenge. As a high-ranking Paxton executive, it was entirely conceivable that she had access to some kind of information that she could use against Isaac.

Sterling's motive, on the other hand, appeared to be simply proactive. All he wanted was to protect his company's and his shareholder's interests. There was nothing bad or harmful about hiring an auditor, like herself, to check and recheck the accounting records. In fact, it was the smart thing to do.

Sterling had told her that he opted not to bring his fears to the attention of the accounting firm that was already on retainer. Autumn knew that if they were doing their jobs—and probably being paid millions in fees to do it—they would have already discovered something was wrong.

Still, maybe they had found something and informed Sterling, but Autumn doubted it because he had given her nothing to go on but a hunch and some old files.

If Felicia had proof of fraud, did she share it with Sterling and all Autumn had to do was find it and vet it? Or were father and daughter each working alone?

And here she was caught in the middle, not making

millions in fees but instead dreaming about Isaac making love to her. If anything, last night was proof that her motives were definitely in the wrong place.

Autumn swung her legs off the bed. Things were moving too quickly between her and Isaac. She had to put a stop to it. Before she fell in love with him and couldn't let go.

Her work had always come first. Her dedication to rooting out the corporate bad guys was what kept her getting up in the morning and why her clients kept calling.

She'd inherited the cop gene from her father, a well-respected New York City detective, who had also graciously bestowed on her the tenacious work ethic that had eventually driven her mother away. Her father had been divorced for over twenty years and, from what she gathered, was happy living alone.

Autumn had never been married and the dates were few and far between. For years, plunging headfirst into case after case had always kept her from feeling she was missing out. Until last night, when Isaac showed her so lovingly what she had been missing. She could only imagine what it would be like for him to completely own her—body and soul.

Her mind knew what she had to do, but her heart wanted something different. It felt like lead in her chest, and at that moment she didn't even want to get out of bed.

Autumn recalled her surprise at learning he was a father and she wondered why he'd decided to adopt instead of marrying and having some children of his own. Adolescents and teens were difficult to place with adoptive families. The majority of them wanted newborn babies, so abandoned teens often went through their entire lives in foster homes.

Yet, Isaac had welcomed them into his home. He was a good person and she respected that he was obviously trying to be a good father to his children. If Isaac was engaged in fraud, they had nothing to do with it. They'd only be victims of the fallout.

Isaac's secret was safe with her, but she felt a pang of guilt knowing that keeping his secrets would help her continue to gain his trust. That's what a good undercover investigator was supposed to do. Work to gain the alleged perpetrator's trust over time, and when enough evidence was gathered, move in for the kill.

For this case, time was working against her, but her growing feelings for Isaac were, too. She was really starting to care about him. How was she going to put all that aside?

The only way to avoid both of them getting hurt was to wrap up the case as quickly as possible. Starting today, she was devoting herself again to her own personal work ethic: no more fun and no more pleasure. By this time next week, she'd be on a plane on her way to her next client. Why start something that only had to end?

Autumn slipped out of bed and padded into the bathroom, intent on a hot shower and a strong cup of tea afterward. Both should make trying to find something to ruin Isaac's life go down a little bit easier.

* * *

Two floors up, Isaac slept soundly, oblivious to everything but his dreams where his mouth was sealed on Autumn's wet flesh, his tongue probing and searching, as she bucked in his arms. Her screams broke through the fog and he awoke with a start.

He propped himself up on his elbows and cursed. He was hard as a rock and the woman who'd made him that way wasn't there.

Reality sucks, he thought, just as the door suddenly opened. His head snapped up to see Devon barreling through his bedroom at high speed. Just before he pounced on the bed, Isaac had the foresight and the quick reflexes to bring his knees to his chest. Otherwise, his ability to have children of his own would have been seriously compromised.

"Hey, Dad!" he shouted.

He grabbed at his son and put him into a loose headlock. "What up, D?" Isaac responded with a smile. "Are you practicing to be a linebacker?"

"No, just trying to wake you up." He laughed as the two play wrestled for a few minutes.

Isaac bopped Devon on the head with a pillow. "You're just about the most dangerous alarm clock on earth. I'm not even about to hit the snooze button!" he joked.

Devon grabbed the pillow from Isaac's hand and bopped him back. "What are we going to do today?"

Isaac held in a smile. That was his children's second favorite question. The first was, *What are we having for dinner?*

"You promised we'd do something fun today, remember?"

All Isaac remembered was that his laptop bag, still where he left it in the foyer, contained a ton of work that had to be completed sometime over the weekend. Not to mention the work he had to do on the Witterman pitch. He couldn't let Autumn do everything, plus it would give him an excuse to see her again.

"I don't know about today, Devon. I've got a ton of work I need to catch up on."

"But, Dad, you promised."

Isaac started to shake his head no but stopped when he saw the look of disappointment on Devon's face. He was still getting used to the fact that he wanted the memories of his children to be so much better than his own.

"What's the weather like?"

Like his kids, Isaac wasn't going down without a fight. Devon jumped out of the bed, parted the curtains and peered out the window. "It looks cold, but at least it's not snowing."

He stifled a groan.

Kid 1—Parent 0.

The temperature he could deal with, but he hated the snow. Trudging around the city battling millions of white flakes, as beautiful as they were, was not his idea of fun. Although he would love to have a snowball fight with his kids one day.

As a foster kid himself, he'd missed out on all kinds of silly but memorable things. But more importantly, he missed out on the unconditional love of a parent.

He'd always wanted two, would have settled for one, but ended up getting none.

Thankfully, something within him, some kind of inner strength helped him hold on. He'd made it through his lonely and often chaotic childhood, graduated at the top of his class at Harvard and was now considered a "success."

Not bad for someone most thought would never even graduate from high school.

Being a foster kid with no one to love and no one to truly love him had affected him. It had made him tough in the wrong place, his heart.

Although Isaac was a single parent, the one thing besides money that his kids would never have to worry about was love.

He couldn't say the same for himself.

Last night, he realized how much he needed a woman in his life and how much he wanted that woman to be Autumn.

Suddenly, he had an idea.

"Devon, go grab my wallet off the dresser."

The boy retrieved the wallet and brought it back to Isaac. He fished out a one hundred dollar bill and gave it to Devon, who stared at it, his eyes like saucers.

"Go down to the flower shop on the corner and get me the biggest bouquet they've got. You can keep the change."

Devon nodded and was out of the room almost as fast as he'd come into it.

"And put your coat on before you leave," Isaac yelled. "We're about to go on an adventure."

Isaac only hoped that the trip would pay off.

Autumn had just poured her second cup of tea when she heard a sharp knock at the door. She ignored it because, in her heart, she knew it was Isaac.

She'd hoped that she would have some time to craft a plausible excuse of why they had to back off from each other. But she knew the reason was right in front of her.

Her heart raced as her eyes skittered to the kitchen table where Isaac's old files were spread out in plain sight. To have to collect and hide them would put her behind on the audit again. But she couldn't let him see them, either.

There was no way she was letting Isaac into her apartment.

The knocking was louder now, though, and more urgent. Isaac or whoever was out there was not going to go away.

She slowly moved to the door and looked through the peephole, breathing a sigh of relief that no one was there.

Just as she turned and was about to walk away, another knock sounded. She opened the door and, instead of Isaac, there was Devon with a bashful grin on his face and a big bouquet of flowers in his hand.

"Wow!" she exclaimed, when he didn't say anything. "Are those for me?"

"Yeah," Devon responded, shoving them forward so hard he almost punched her in the stomach by accident.

Autumn sidestepped Devon's fist and took the collection of roses, daisies and snapdragons decorated with ferns and baby's breath. A few of the ribbons that held the bunch together were so long they almost trailed to the floor and she realized they must have come loose somehow.

She buried her face in the bouquet and inhaled the incredible scents. "They're beautiful, thank you!"

Devon bowed awkwardly. "My father requests the pleasure of your company at our afternoon adventure."

Autumn raised an eyebrow. "Adventure? Where are we going?"

He straightened and shrugged. "I don't know. But my dad is rich, so it could be anywhere." Autumn heard the excitement in his voice, and she wondered if he knew how fortunate he was to have a father like Isaac.

She leaned against the doorway, knowing that she didn't have it in her to refuse. Flowers were her weakness.

"He's also very sweet. Please tell him that I accept his invitation," Autumn replied, her nose still in the flowers.

"Okay. Meet us in the lobby at 1:00 p.m. sharp. Later, yo!"

"Later!" she called after Devon, who was already down the hall and getting into the elevator.

Autumn closed the door and walked into the kitchen, where Isaac's files were practically calling her name. She didn't want to know what was in there even though she'd been hired to find out.

But wherever they were going this afternoon, maybe

Isaac would reveal something that could help her investigation so that she could say goodbye before either of them got hurt.

Or maybe spending a Saturday afternoon with Isaac would make her fall in love with him. She plunged her nose into the bouquet again, inhaling the scent not of flowers, but of fear.

Chapter 9

Autumn spent another hour poring over files, trying her best to concentrate and failing miserably. Every few minutes she would glance over at the flowers, now sitting in a vase on her kitchen counter, wondering what was behind Isaac's kind gesture other than the fact that he'd sent his son to deliver them.

She hated that she was being so suspicious, but it came with the territory. Her undercover work investigating corporate criminals so they could be brought to justice didn't exactly inspire instant trust.

And while she wanted to believe that the same man who denied his own needs to pleasure her all night and then had flowers delivered in the morning was innocent of any wrongdoing, all of it could be a ruse.

Until her investigation was complete, she resolved

again to be on her guard for any sign of an ulterior motive.

With his searing touch and mind-blowing kisses she swore she could still feel, Isaac had already proved how easily he could melt her ironclad will.

I'll just have to be stronger, she vowed as she cleared the kitchen table. The files had revealed nothing, but she was convinced she was missing something or maybe she just didn't want to see it. Even more reason to let things cool with Isaac.

After changing into her favorite skinny jeans and dressy top, she pulled on her black leather boots. The heels weren't too high, so she wouldn't almost fall on her face on the ice like she had so embarrassingly the other night when Isaac had kissed her for the first time.

Autumn donned her pale blue cashmere peacoat and pulled a wool hat over her curly hair. She clutched the handrail as she rode the elevator downstairs, her heart thumping in anticipation of seeing Isaac again. Her heels tapped on the marble floor as she walked to the front of the lobby.

When she arrived, she saw Isaac speaking to the doorman and she brought her hands to her chest in fear. Hopefully, he wasn't telling Isaac about how she was bribing him for information. When he tipped his hat in Autumn's direction, Isaac quickly ended his conversation and greeted her with a lazy smile that made her heart flip.

"Hello, stranger. Long time no see."

Isaac strolled over, so sexy in dark indigo jeans, a white button-down shirt and a black leather coat that looked buttery soft. She gulped down a breath trying to forget how much she wanted to explore him and the searing orgasms he'd given her only hours earlier.

He reached for her arm and leaned in close. "You're still as beautiful as ever."

The heat of his touch radiated through the heavy fabric of her coat. She started to wrap her arms around his waist, but out of the corner of her eye, she saw his two children lift their heads from their phones.

Her cheeks burned. "Thank you," she whispered, hoping she didn't sound out of breath. Isaac had heard her gasping enough last evening.

Autumn took a quick step back as his children approached.

Devon gave her a friendly wave. He had a round face that always looked cheerful. Deshauna wore a nasty glare that almost made Autumn cringe and wonder if accepting Isaac's invitation was a huge mistake.

Spending the afternoon with two teenagers and their mind-blowingly hot dad. What was she getting herself into?

Despite her jitters, she gave both kids a warm smile.

"Where are we going?" Devon asked, addressing his question to her.

Autumn shrugged. "Your guess is as good as mine."

"How about we just stay home," Deshauna said sulkily, still glaring at Autumn. "Whose dumb idea was this anyway? It's freezing outside!"

"The cold air is invigorating," Isaac interjected. "It'll give you guys plenty of energy to tackle your homework later on tonight."

Both kids groaned. They had started to pull out their devices in defeat when the doorman walked up and cleared his throat.

"Your car is ready, sir."

Devon ran to the lobby door and pushed it open. "That's not a car. That's a limo!" he said, his voice cracking with excitement.

"Sweet," Deshauna said. Her face brightened as she stepped outside and got her first look at the sleek black vehicle.

"Can we get in now, Dad?" Devon asked. The chauffeur opened the door and Devon was in the limo before Isaac could respond.

Deshauna stepped in next and plopped down next to her brother. She immediately went to the minirefrigerator and grabbed a can of soda as if she'd ridden in a limo a million times.

Autumn ducked in advance of the low ceiling and could feel Isaac watching her climb in. His eyes met hers briefly as he slid into the seat beside her.

"Dad, can I have one of these for prom next year?" Deshauna asked, after a sip of soda.

Devon was busy pressing every button he could see. "Can we keep it?"

Isaac laughed. "No, we can't keep it. It's just a rental. But we can have fun in it today. Only the best for my family."

Both kids pouted for a few seconds but then forgot about the sulkies as they checked out the limo's luxurious features.

Autumn quietly inhaled the smell of Isaac's cologne

through her nostrils. The scent was even stronger now that they were in closer quarters. Not overpoweringly so, but just enough to make her want to bury her head in his neck. Like forever.

After a ride through Central Park, the limo emerged onto Fifth Avenue and parked in front of the Metropolitan Museum of Art.

"Dad," Devon whined as he clambered out after his sister. "I thought you said you were taking us on an adventure."

Autumn was equally surprised at Isaac's choice for a Saturday outing. She thought for sure they were headed to something more testosterone based, like a hockey game or maybe even bowling. Isaac never failed to intrigue her, and strange as it might seem, his being into art was a turn-on. She couldn't wait to explore the museum with him at her side.

By the time Isaac climbed out of the limo, Devon and Deshauna had already started up the stairs to the entrance. "This place has something from every culture in every part of the world. You don't call that an adventure?" he called out after them.

He reached for her hand and held it tight as he helped her from the limo. Their eyes locked and his smile warmed her in a way that made her feel she was curled up in his arms. And Lord help her, she wished that she could be.

The wind whipped her curls across her face and Isaac gently brushed them away with his right hand.

He stepped closer and cupped her chin lightly, as if he was going to kiss her.

"I'm glad you're here."

Her heart fluttered in her chest, and for a moment she didn't speak—she just panicked. She wanted him to kiss her but not in front of his children. She didn't want it to appear as if she and Isaac were in a relationship when they were really just friends. If he ever found out she was investigating him, they'd turn into enemies real quick.

Autumn stepped back far enough that it forced him to drop his hand from her face.

"So am I," she admitted truthfully as she withdrew her hand from his.

She hugged her arms around her chest and shivered. "Let's get inside. It's freezing out here."

Isaac nodded and they walked up the stairs to the museum, where they met up with Devon and Deshauna.

Once inside, Autumn gaped at the immensity of the lobby area while Isaac went to pay the admission fee. Although hundreds of people milled about, it didn't seem at all crowded.

Isaac returned shortly and after they checked their coats in, he handed each of them a paper ticket.

"Peel the sticker off carefully and stick it to your shirt," he instructed.

He then gave Devon and Deshauna one map to share and kept the other one for himself.

Isaac unfolded the map and Autumn held one corner of it so that she could look at it, too.

"Where would you guys like to go first?"

Devon piped up first. "Arms and Armor!"

"Boys and guns. So typical!" Deshauna muttered and rolled her eyes. "I want to see the costume exhibit."

"That sounds like fun. I love fashion, too," Autumn said in a friendly tone.

Deshauna clicked her tongue against her teeth and gave her a nasty look. "What do you know about style?" she retorted in a snippy voice.

Isaac's head snapped up. "Chill out, Deshauna. Autumn is our guest today and you will treat her with respect. Is that clear?"

Deshauna slanted her eyes in Autumn's direction and nodded reluctantly.

Poor kid, Autumn thought. Deshauna obviously felt threatened by Autumn for her father's affections. She wished she could reassure her that she had no need to worry. Autumn knew she would never have a permanent place in Isaac's heart.

Isaac turned to Autumn. "What would you like to see?"

She quickly perused the map. "I'd love to see any paintings and sculpture from Europe."

Deshauna took the map from her brother and folded it. "Dad, can we split up?"

Devon nodded. "Yeah, can we?"

Isaac frowned. "I was hoping we'd explore the museum as a family."

"We'll be good, we promise," Deshauna replied in a sweet voice before elbowing her brother. "Won't we?"

"Ouch!" Devon rubbed his side. "Yeah. So what do you say, Dad?"

Isaac sighed. "Okay, but be sure and stay with your

sister. Let's all meet back here in an hour and we can check out some of the other exhibits together."

His children didn't even wait for him to finish his sentence before they half walked, half jogged away.

Isaac turned to Autumn. "So much for a family outing," he said with a dejected shrug.

"They're teenagers. Don't take it to heart. When I was their age, I didn't want to hang out with my dad either."

They walked to the escalator that would take them to the second floor where some of the Met's vast collection of European paintings were located.

"What does your father do?" Isaac asked as they rode. "Does he work with money all day long like we do?" he teased.

Autumn hesitated a moment, unsure whether to answer what was otherwise a normal question. Even though she knew Isaac would be unable to trace her real identity, she was still fearful. To her, that was just another indication that she still wasn't used to her new life. But even if she could, she wouldn't change a thing. Her former employer's fraudulent accounting practices had bilked thousands of shareholders out of millions of dollars. Exposing these actions had cost Autumn her name, her reputation and career, but it had ultimately led her to Isaac.

"No. He busts bad guys for a living."

She paused a beat, watching Isaac's face for any kind of unusual reaction, but there was none, and she exhaled lightly with relief. "He's been a detective for the borough of Manhattan for over twenty years."

"Well, I hope if I ever meet him, he's not packing metal," Isaac joked.

His broad smile turned grim and his voice was so low Autumn could barely hear him.

"Unlike my son, I don't have a fascination with guns. I don't have anything against them. It's just that when I was growing up, they almost destroyed my life."

Isaac's stark honesty made Autumn's heart squeeze and her legs felt shaky when they disembarked from the escalator.

Without speaking, they wandered through the gallery and gazed at the priceless European paintings, both hoping that the other would break the uncomfortable calm between them.

Finally, Autumn reached out her hand and grasped Isaac's arm.

"Do you want to tell me what happened?" she asked softly.

Isaac looked around, as if to make sure his kids or any other people weren't in earshot.

"My father shot my mother and then killed himself."

His response was blunt, yet it didn't detract from the unmistakable pain etched in his eyes.

Horrified, Autumn breathed in so sharply and loudly that a few people in the room turned in her direction.

Without thinking, Autumn wrapped her arms around Isaac's neck.

"Oh, my God, Isaac. I'm so sorry," she managed to choke out.

He shrugged nonchalantly, linking his arms around her waist. "That's how I ended up being a foster kid.

And when I learned that the same thing had happened to Devon and Deshauna's birth parents when they were little, I adopted them. No kid should have to go through life alone."

She hugged Isaac even tighter, as if doing so could erase anything bad that had happened, and she realized just how much she was starting to care about him.

"I think what you did for Devon and Deshauna is amazing," she whispered into his ear. "You're a very special man."

Autumn knew adoption took a certain kind of selflessness. Plus Devon and Deshauna were victims of the same unconscionable violence he'd experienced as a kid. Raising them had to bring back painful memories of his own traumatic childhood.

She squeezed him even harder. How was he coping?

"Hey, go easy on the neck," he said tersely, disentangling himself from her grasp. "I can barely breathe."

Autumn dropped her arms to her sides. Her face prickled with embarrassment. What had caused her to hold on to him so tightly that she didn't want to let go? It was crazy. Especially when she knew very well that any kind of relationship with him was not only temporary—it was a mistake.

"Sorry," she muttered. "I was just trying to make you feel better."

Isaac sighed and ran one hand down his face. "No, I'm the one who should be sorry. I didn't mean to bite your head off."

Autumn nodded and started walking away, pretending to be deeply curious about the paintings that lined the wall.

Pretending she wasn't falling in love with Isaac.

She stopped in front of *Venus and Adonis*. She read the little sign on the wall and learned that it was a work by Peter Paul Rubens, a Flemish artist who lived during the late 1500s, early 1600s.

Isaac caught up to her and before he could say anything more, she pointed at the painting. "That's Adonis to the left. He's the god of beauty. Venus, the god of love, is to his right. Little Cupid is holding on to Adonis's leg."

"The chubby little guy probably wants his bow and arrow back," Isaac joked.

Autumn rolled her eyes. "I took an art history class in college and I remember that my instructor taught us that this painting is about Venus trying to prevent her lover, Adonis, from going into battle." She paused and shrugged. "Or maybe it was hunting. I forget."

"Why would she do that? The man was probably trying to put food on the table for his family."

She crossed her arms and looked deeply into his eyes. "Because she didn't want him to get hurt."

"So what happened?"

"According to myth, he ignores her pleas and ends up getting killed by a wild boar."

"Wow." Isaac shook his head. "I guess he should have listened to his woman."

They both stared at the painting for a moment.

Venus, her skin milky-white, her form Rubenesque. In today's world, she would be called fat, but Autumn thought she was beautiful. Adonis, clad in an orangish-red tunic, with his long hair and thickly muscled body, was a mythological romance hero. Their figures twisting into each other, toward a fate that was at that point unknown.

Isaac suddenly turned to her. "Will you be my Venus?"

Autumn felt her skin prickle at the heat of his gaze. "Do you mean your lover or your protector?"

He put his hands on her shoulders and touched his forehead to hers. "Both. I want to make love to you, Autumn," he said softly. "And in the morning, I want you to hold on to me tight, like you did a moment ago."

"Before you go into battle?" she whispered. At his nod, she asked, "What are you fighting against, Isaac?"

"Certainly not wild boars. Sometimes I think I'm fighting against nothing. Sometimes I think I'm fighting against myself." He paused and when he spoke again, his low voice caressed her ear. "I want you, Autumn. Last night was wonderful, but it wasn't enough for me. Not even close."

Autumn bit her lip and looked up at him. "I want to...but we work together. Things could get complicated very quickly. If Sterling or Felicia ever—"

Isaac laid his finger on her lips. "Shh...they won't. We'll be careful. I promise." He kissed her forehead. "Just think about it, okay?"

She nodded and moved her hands up his muscular back and clung to his shoulder blades as he kissed her nose and finally her mouth. Tilting her body against his as he stroked her hair, she opened her heart to him and, in her mind, they were alone as one. In those moments, she felt as priceless as the paintings on the wall.

Isaac's phone buzzed and reluctantly they drew apart. He ran his thumb over the screen. "It's Deshauna. They're downstairs waiting for us by the escalator."

She looked up at him, her lips still burning from his kisses, her mind in a whirl. "I guess we'd better go meet them."

As they made their way to the escalator, the floor seemed to be swaying dizzily under her feet and she stopped, trying to gain her footing.

Isaac, thinking she was right behind him, had already started to descend. When he noticed she wasn't there, he turned around and bolted up the moving stairs.

Autumn stepped back from the escalator. "I don't know why, but I'm feeling a little disoriented."

"I'll help you." He stretched out his hand. "Just grab me and hold on tight."

His hand clasped hers, its masculine grip so warm and strong that Autumn felt nothing bad could ever happen to them. But as they stepped onto the escalator together, she knew she was wrong, and that whatever she decided would only result in one thing: heartbreak.

Chapter 10

Isaac stifled a yawn and leaned back in his chair, trying to decide which was worse. An eight o'clock meeting on a Monday morning or a meeting with Felicia. Unfortunately, he was experiencing both.

His eyes drifted around the room and he noted that there were people from all levels of the organization in attendance. He wondered how many of them really wanted to be there. While participation was "voluntary," the unspoken word was that if you were invited yet didn't show up, you were not a team player. At least in Felicia's eyes.

The same verdict held true if a man, namely him, refused her advances.

Felicia rapped her pen on the boardroom table and

called the inaugural meeting of the Paxton Employee Satisfaction Committee to order.

Isaac straightened but pressed his back into the chair. This was one meeting that he wished he hadn't been invited to.

"Ladies and gentlemen," she began. "I've called us together this morning because it has come to my attention that we have a serious morale issue at Paxton that needs to be addressed." She paused and let her gaze roam around the table. "This committee is going to be responsible for brainstorming ways to fix these issues so that all employees will be happy in their careers at Paxton."

Isaac stared straight ahead and pretended to be engrossed in whatever Felicia was rambling on about next, but his mind was on Autumn.

The kiss they shared at the art museum had done more than just stimulate his body. It also made him think.

Oh…the possibility that he could have Autumn. It wasn't just the physical stuff, although that was very important to him. It was everything else that he wanted to share with her but didn't know where to start.

He hadn't been this excited about the future since he'd started at Paxton, fresh out of Harvard with no goal other than to make money, and lots of it.

Now, he had the money and two kids to share it with. But he knew that wasn't enough. He wanted a partner, a woman who was committed to a career and to building a life with him. The only thing he didn't know was if Autumn wanted the same thing.

He'd meant to sneak out of his apartment on Saturday evening sometime, but Devon got sick soon after they arrived back from the museum. Thankfully, he felt better on Sunday. But by then both kids were busy trying to avoid doing homework, so he spent most of the day encouraging and monitoring them through it while catching up on work of his own.

Now, Isaac was stuck in the meeting from hell.

All of a sudden, he noticed the room was totally silent and everyone in it was staring at him.

His back went ramrod straight, having no idea what was going on.

"Can you repeat the question?" he ventured.

Nobody spoke for a moment and all that could be heard was the faint sound of traffic fifty stories below.

"So let me bring you up to speed," Felicia said scathingly. "We were discussing some of our employees' biggest complaints."

She pointed to a man sitting right across from Isaac. He worked for the information technology department, informally known as PGS, Paxton Geek Squad. Mostly he answered help desk calls, but occasionally when things were really busy, Isaac had seen him around the office troubleshooting and fixing computer issues.

"Jonathan was inquiring why a new employee analyst was given an office when most people, other than executives, are assigned to a cubicle."

It was obvious that Felicia was referring to Autumn having the office across from his, a fact over which he had no control. Still he was secretly glad she was there and as far as he was concerned, he didn't want her to move.

Isaac narrowed his eyes. What did she have up her sleeve now?

Jonathan fiddled with his tie. "Y-yes," he stammered, looking down at the table. "People are upset. It's not f-fair."

Isaac leaned forward in his chair. "I can't answer that question for you. I'm not responsible for work space arrangements." He turned to Felicia. "Quite frankly, I'm confused as to why this issue even concerns me."

"Because our employees have the perception that our executive team has special privileges, which could be why morale is lower at the company overall."

Isaac opened his mouth to argue, but he quickly shut it as he realized what was happening here. Felicia was trying to pin the blame on him for two things that were out of his control: office morale and Autumn's work space.

Isaac glanced around at the other employees sitting at the table; some he knew, but most he didn't. Many of them wouldn't even look him in the eye. What kind of lies had Felicia been feeding them?

He wouldn't be surprised if she'd met with each person secretly to come up with some kind of accusation to level at him.

There was no way he was going to be a punching bag for their frustrations.

He took a deep breath. "Look, I don't know why morale is down at Paxton. In terms of perks, there is nothing unusual outside of my compensation package, which is, of course, strictly confidential."

Felicia cut in. "This isn't the place to—"

"Let me finish please," Isaac said. "If you are personally unsatisfied in your job, voicing your complaints in a meeting such as this isn't going to help. Review what you want, compare it against what's lacking in your job, and discuss your concerns with your supervisor. Otherwise, this committee is little more than a group gossip session."

When Isaac was finished, he saw a few heads nodding in agreement. Felicia glared at him, but addressed the group.

"Thank you for that insightful career advice. We'll adjourn the meeting for now and reconvene next week."

Not if I can help it, he thought, as people began filing out of the room.

As he stood up to make his own escape, his phone vibrated, a signal that his next meeting was due to begin shortly. If he hurried, he could go see if Autumn was in the office yet.

When Isaac walked by Felicia, she reached out her hand and touched him on his arm. Revulsion sifted through him. Despite his anger, somehow he managed to keep his tone light.

"What is it? Haven't you done enough to try to ruin my day?"

Isaac was beyond tired of Felicia's little games and they had to stop. It was time he took his own advice. He had to go to Sterling with his concerns. But he couldn't until after the Witterman pitch. It was more important than ever that he win the business. Maybe then, after signing the elusive multimillion dollar prospective client, Sterling would listen to him.

Felicia tossed her blond hair to one side. "All is fair in love and war." She squeezed his forearm and her voice was razor sharp. "And if I can't have love, then…"

Isaac didn't give her a chance to finish her sentence. He surmised what Felicia was hinting at even though she let it dangle. He shook his arm free from her grasp and strode out of the door.

If this was war, then Isaac knew he needed to prepare for a battle. He hurried down the hall in search of the only person he wanted by his side.

Autumn sat alone at a table in the corner of the Paxton cafeteria, nestling a fresh cup of tea in her hands. Her thoughts were a whirlwind of Isaac, the investigation and something else she couldn't quite pinpoint.

She stared down at the white plastic lid and realized how fluid and simple her life was now. She could go anywhere. Do anything. With her government-issued identity, she had no past and no future. She had only the present.

Yet, like the liquid in her cup, she was constrained. By virtue of necessity, whether it was for a particular case or for her own protection, she was held back from doing what she loved out in the open. In the pursuit of the truth, her real self was hidden from others. Her biggest fear was that someday she would look in the mirror and she wouldn't recognize the person staring back.

With a sigh, Autumn brought the cup to her lips and

her stomach clenched when she noticed Sterling walk through the cafeteria door heading for her.

"We need to talk," he ordered, pulling out a chair opposite her own.

Although there was no one sitting within hearing distance, several people glanced in her direction. Autumn made a mental note to remind him that they needed to meet in his office from now on.

Autumn took a sip of tea and set it down, unperturbed at Sterling's gruff tone.

"How was your weekend?"

"I was here the entire time, but never mind that," he retorted. "I stopped by your office on Sunday and saw that some of the files were missing. Do you have them?"

"Yes," she replied. "I took them home to review them over the weekend. Why?"

"The Witterman pitch is this Friday. I had high hopes that you would have found something by now," he sneered. "I guess I was wasting my time…and my money."

Autumn tightened her grip around the cup, bristling inwardly at Sterling's implication that she wasn't doing her job, when nothing could be further from the truth.

She'd combed through Isaac's files and client records, dating back to when he started with the company, and she only had a small batch to go.

The time she'd spent with Isaac these past few days were a part of her surveillance efforts. She was supposed to get to know him, closely monitor every move of his taut, muscular body and record any and all interactions with him.

But I wasn't supposed to fall in love with him.

A burst of panic made her grip the cup tighter. The thought seemed so loud in her mind that for a moment she feared Sterling could hear it. The notion that she could have any feelings for Isaac beyond simple lust was highly illogical, not to mention potentially detrimental to the case.

She couldn't ever record how Isaac had pleasured her in her apartment a few nights earlier, although the memory was forever seared in her brain. She couldn't stop thinking about him, and yet she wasn't supposed to be thinking about him.

Not like that anyway.

"It's not because I haven't been looking," she insisted, trying her best not to squirm under Sterling's harsh glare. "Are you sure you've given me every file?"

Sterling cast her a withering look. "Are you questioning the way I run my business and accusing me of losing crucial information?"

Autumn held up her hands. "Not at all. I was just putting it out there. Things happen sometimes, that's all."

He crossed his arms and huffed. "Not at Paxton, they don't."

Autumn nodded. "Initially you refused to tell me why you were having Isaac investigated in the first place."

Sterling wrinkled his forehead. "What difference does that make?"

Autumn flashed him a smile even though she wanted to gag. For a man responsible for the care and feeding of millions of other people's money, Sterling sure didn't have much common sense.

"Knowing all the facts could assist the investigation," she replied patiently.

Sterling unfolded his arms and leaned close to her. "Let me tell you something, Ms. Hilliard. When I invest money in a particular stock, I don't know all the facts."

He coughed and continued. "Sure, I can read the prospectus and see how the company has fared over a certain period of time, but in the end, investing is a high-stakes guessing game. I'm working off a hunch and I've made a living hedging bets."

At his words, the bitter acid from the tea rose in Autumn's throat. Didn't Sterling realize that there was more at stake here than money? There was Isaac's career and the children no one at Paxton knew about except her.

"And what if you're wrong? About Isaac, I mean."

Sterling opened his arms wide, as if he were Moses parting the Red Sea. "Look around you, Autumn. Does it look like I'm ever wrong?"

Autumn coughed back her disgust. "No, sir."

"Good." Sterling dropped his arms and stood. "I've got another meeting. But I expect a full report from you no later than a week from today."

He took a few steps but suddenly turned back. "Oh, and by the way, when you discover that my hunch is correct, Isaac is going to wish he never set foot inside these doors."

Autumn slumped in her seat, knowing his threat was genuine.

Obviously Sterling had never heard of the maxim "innocent until proven guilty."

She wondered what had caused so much friction between them, but it didn't matter at the moment. Her father told her repeatedly, "You're only as good as your last case, so..."

"Don't burn bridges," she muttered, echoing her dad's solemn voice in her head.

Her reputation and her career mattered more to Autumn than a man. Or at least, that's what she told herself, every night she turned on her side and no one was there.

Autumn got up and walked over to the garbage can. As she tossed in her empty cup, she vowed to set aside the romantic feelings for Isaac that had already started to grow inside her. At least for now, and perhaps, forever.

Later that morning, Autumn walked out of the restroom, drying her hands on a paper towel, and nearly bumped into Felicia. However, from the fake surprise look on her face, Autumn knew the chance meeting was no accident.

"I'm glad to see someone at Paxton taking hand washing seriously."

Autumn balled up the paper towel in her hand and shrugged. "I'm not a germaphobe. It's just good hygiene."

Felicia clapped her hands together. "I knew we had something else in common." She produced a small bottle and held it out to her. "Sanitizer? It's lavender scented."

Autumn shook her head and felt like telling Felicia to use it on herself, even though no amount of the clear gel would be able to wash off the sleaze.

"I'm glad we ran into each other." Something flashed in Felicia's eyes and Autumn instantly knew she was lying. "Do you have time for a chat?"

Without waiting for Autumn's response, Felicia grabbed her elbow and pulled her into a room that was reserved for nursing mothers. Luckily, it was occupied only by a couch that appeared sturdy though in need of newer upholstery.

Felicia locked the door and gestured to the sofa.

Autumn shook her head. "I'll stand. What's going on?"

"I just wanted to say that whatever you're doing, keep doing it. The natives are restless!" she squealed.

"Natives?" Autumn echoed, confused. "What are you talking about?"

Felicia rolled her eyes. "I'm talking about the fact that we had our inaugural meeting of the Paxton Employee Satisfaction Committee. Everyone is up in arms about the fact that you have an office."

Autumn dropped her mouth open. "But, Felicia, you know I had nothing to do with that. Your father gave me that office."

"I know and initially I was really upset about it," Felicia admitted. "But now it seems to be working to your advantage. Everyone is blaming Isaac, which is exactly what I want."

Despite her will to stand, Autumn found herself sinking to the couch. "But why? It's not his fault, either."

"That's where you're wrong," Felicia replied, turning to the mirror. She smoothed a hand over her blond hair. Today, her style was less severe, but the calculated smirk on her face was all that was needed to make Autumn's stomach knot with worry.

What had Isaac done to make Felicia so vindictive?

"Do you know how long it took me to get my own office?"

Autumn shook her head and resumed watching Felicia primp in the mirror.

"Three years." Felicia turned on her heels and held up her fingers. "Three years! And I'm the boss's daughter!" she exclaimed. "I know what people say about me, but it's not true."

"So your father has made you work to get where you are today."

"Yes," Felicia cut in. "I followed in his hallowed footsteps and now I can barely get him to answer an email."

Autumn ignored the long look on her face. If Felicia wanted sympathy, she wasn't going to get it from her.

"What's that got to do with Isaac?"

Felicia put her hands on her hips. "Let's just say that when I get through with Isaac, he won't be able to show his face ever again in Manhattan."

Without another word, Felicia unlocked the door and stalked out.

Autumn rubbed her eyes in confusion. To her, Felicia's mini-rant sounded a bit like professional jealousy. But since Isaac was involved somehow, this was a lot more complex than mere envy. She had to find out what, if anything beyond her attempt at seduction, had occurred between them.

And even though Autumn couldn't claim Isaac as her man, she had to do it without getting jealous herself.

Chapter 11

Isaac hurried down the hallway toward Autumn's office, hoping to catch her before she left. He'd been wanting to see her, but meetings had kept him busy all day and he kept missing her. What he had to say couldn't be done in an email. He needed to be close to her, perhaps for the very last time.

When he arrived, he stopped just before the thin floor-to-ceiling window and inclined his head. The door was closed, but he could hear the faint tap of her fingers upon the keys. He took a deep breath and knocked on the door before opening it.

He popped his head into the room. Autumn looked up and her lips curved under the spotlight cast by the old-fashioned desk lamp. As she leaned back against her chair, her face was thrown into semidarkness but, thankfully, her smile was still there. His heart lifted as if it was eighty degrees and sunny rather than the frigid cold that awaited them both outside.

"Hey, it's after five. I thought you'd be gone by now."

Autumn shook her head and motioned him forward. "I just finished the presentation and was trying to email it to you, but it bounced back."

"Hmm…maybe I can help."

He stepped into the room and closed the door. "You wouldn't know it by looking at me, but I'm a closet geek."

Autumn gave him a quizzical look and her eyes zeroed in on his chest. He took a deep breath as his skin warmed under her gaze.

"Oh really? Where's your pocket protector?" she teased.

Isaac felt her eyes on his body as he walked around her desk. He placed his hands on the back of her chair.

"I could tell you," he replied, standing behind her before swiveling the chair so she faced him. "Or I could show you." Isaac watched her eyes flick down and graze over his torso. The moment lasted only seconds, but it was enough to make him hard. His penis throbbed and his mind warned him to back away from this woman, but his body yearned for something else.

He stepped closer, placed his hands on the armrests of the chair and bent at the waist.

"Which would you like?"

Her eyes rose, darkened and met his.

He sensed that she wanted him, but something was holding her back.

She folded her arms as if to ward him off or maybe to stem the flow of her own feelings. "What I want is to get the presentation to you without it blowing up my system."

"Why don't we go over it together? I could order in some dinner and—"

Autumn shook her head. "What about your children? Don't you have to get home to feed them?"

He released his grip on the chair. "First of all, they hate when I cook. They go into hiding when they hear me in the kitchen."

Autumn giggled. "That bad, huh?"

"Unfortunately, yes," Isaac said with a nod. "Second of all, they are with friends tonight." He lifted a tendril of hair from her face. "So I'm all yours."

Her eyes flicked past him to the window. "We may even be snowed in tonight."

Isaac looked over his shoulder and saw a mass of flurries against the glass. He turned and traced a finger along the apple of her cheek. It was as soft as the curve of a pillow.

"Would that be so bad?" he asked.

Autumn's eyes slid shut for a moment as if she were reveling in his touch. "No." Her eyes flapped open and she whispered, "I've missed you."

At those three words, Isaac placed his palms against the cold black leather on either side of her head. The chair rolled back, metal scraping against wood as he engulfed her mouth in a kiss.

Autumn opened her mouth to accept his tongue, her deep moan bubbling into his throat, and he retreated for only a second before plunging and swirling, wanting them to drown in each other.

But it was she who came to her senses first, albeit slowly. Hesitantly. Her palms flattened against his shirt and moved over the hardened muscles, her lips twisting and reaching for him even as she pushed him away.

He stepped back and groaned as he wiped his lips. The emptiness left in his heart by the sudden lack of her touch was something akin to torture.

"Isaac," she began, trying to catch her breath. "We can't do this."

His heart sank and his eyes roamed her face. "You said that you missed me. Did you really mean it?"

"Of course, I did. But before we go any further, we need to talk about Felicia."

Isaac sighed and stepped back. "What do you want to know?"

"What's going on between the two of you?"

He leaned his head back against the wall and stared at the ceiling. "Nothing. But that's not what she wants."

"You told me that she's been making your life at Paxton here a living hell lately."

Isaac leveled his gaze at her and nodded. "I think she's turned Sterling against me. He's not acting the way he normally does with me and he's always in a bad mood."

Autumn twisted her lips to the side. "I thought that was just his personality."

He couldn't help but laugh. "No, not at all. It's just lately he's been treating me differently. More like an outsider than a confidant."

"Don't you think you may be blowing this out of proportion?" Autumn asked gently.

Isaac scratched his chin. "I used to think so until today. Felicia has me on this committee that is supposed to be a nonconfrontational sounding board for employee grievances and how to resolve them, but instead she threw me under the bus. Everyone is blaming me because you have an office, and they don't!"

"I know," Autumn replied quietly.

He pushed himself away from the wall. "You do? How?"

"Felicia told me this morning. She practically accosted me outside the women's restroom."

"That b—" He swallowed the word just in time. "What did she say?"

"The same thing you just told me," Autumn replied, tilting her head. "But with a little added bonus."

Isaac raised his brow, urging her to continue.

"She wanted me to keep an eye on you, and report back anything I find."

"Anything you find? What do I have to hide?" Anger sipped through his veins and he struggled to keep his voice down. "I can't believe she is trying to turn you against me, too."

Autumn clucked her tongue against her teeth. "Really?"

Isaac grunted. "You're right. This is Felicia we're talking about." He shook his head. "You haven't worked here that long and you've already got her pegged for what she is. A sneaky, conniving, little you-know-what who—"

"Has your briefs in a bunch," Autumn cut in. She stood, walked over to the window and faced him. "But what you're not telling me is why all this matters."

"It matters because it's my livelihood," he retorted.

"But you're one of the highest paid and most profitable brokers on Wall Street today. I'm sure you have nothing to worry about."

"Nothing except losing my job." He ran his hand over his head in frustration. "If Sterling or—worse—Felicia, ever finds out that I have two children now, they'll be more than just pissed."

She put her hands on his shoulders. "Isaac, they can't fire you because you adopted two children. I'm not a lawyer, but that sounds like it would be a clear case of discrimination."

Autumn hesitated and he could practically see the wheels turning in her head. "I guess they could reprimand you in some way for withholding information."

"Or find a reason to fire me."

Autumn dropped her hands from his shoulders and leaned against the opposite wall. "The best thing to do would be to tell them about Devon and Deshauna right away."

Isaac paced in front of the window. "But I can't. Not until after I'm made partner. I don't want anything screwing up what I've worked so long and hard to attain."

He snapped his fingers and turned to her. "That's it, isn't it? That's why Felicia asked you to spy on me.

She's building some kind of case against me in order to convince Sterling to let me go. Am I right?"

Autumn shrugged. "I don't know, Isaac. I have no idea what her motives are."

"I do! She's out to destroy me," he insisted as he paced back and forth again.

She reached out her hand and grabbed his arm. "But that's what I'm trying to tell you. She won't. She can't."

He stopped in his tracks. "How do you know?"

"Because I told her no," she said emphatically. "I told her that I refused to spy on you."

Isaac put her hands on Autumn's shoulders and peered into her eyes. "You did?"

She nodded and he pulled her into his arms.

"Thank you. I knew you weren't like everyone else," he whispered against her curls. "So many women I've met in the past were backstabbers. I couldn't trust them with my time, let alone my heart. But you're different. I trust you."

"I'm flattered, Isaac. But you hardly know me. Why me?"

He cupped her chin in one hand. "Maybe it's because Sterling trusted you first. You know the Witterman pitch is a big deal. He wouldn't have given you the assignment if he didn't think you could handle it."

"But, Isaac, that's business," she insisted. "And this is—"

"Personal. I know," he muttered low. He leaned in, took a chance and pecked her lips. "And I want us to get even more personal. So close we won't know where you start and where I end. What do you think?"

"I think we should get back to work on the Witterman presentation."

Isaac groaned and leaned his forehead against hers. "You're no fun."

"But I am efficient and efficiency—"

"Is one spoke in the Paxton wheel of fortune, blah, blah, blah. I can't believe you actually read the employee handbook!"

"Way to kill a moment, huh?" Autumn mused, her eyes twinkling.

Isaac laughed. "Don't worry. If I have anything to say about it, there will be plenty more."

Autumn pulled away and smiled, but he could tell there was something still bothering her. He hoped that in time she would trust him enough to confide in him.

"Why don't you pull that chair around so we can both look at the monitor together?"

Isaac glanced at the door, puzzled. Her drop into business mode was as unexpected as the stock market he played in all day. The trouble was, he knew how to win the market.

He had no clue how to win her.

"But I was going to order in dinner."

"There's no need." Autumn shook her head. "This won't take long. I want you to get home to Devon and Deshauna as soon as possible."

Isaac shrugged, not bothering to remind her that his children were with friends for most of the evening.

He pulled a chair around next to Autumn. Once he was settled in, she put the presentation in full-screen mode and began to walk him through it.

"First, we'll lay some groundwork to make Ms. Witterman comfortable with the organization by reviewing our long history of successful investing, et cetera."

With her right hand, she clicked on the mouse and kept talking, but the only thing Isaac noted was her fingers. They were long, manicured and completely bare. In spite of his fear of the altar, he imagined a ring on one of them. A nice big, ridiculously expensive rock, but not necessarily from him.

Autumn had the kind of raw, earthy, back-to-Eve beauty that a man would have to be a fool to let get away.

She had to have someone in her life.

Suddenly, he felt an elbow in his rib cage.

"Isaac. Are you listening?" Autumn demanded.

His mind drew a blank on everything but her sexy little nose. It had a slight crook in it that he longed to trace with his finger.

"Yeah, I'm down with that," he finally muttered. Although he didn't even know what he'd just agreed to do, he hoped it involved the tearing off of clothes.

She gave him a quizzical look. "So you'll review the accuracy of the corporate backgrounder, correct?"

"Of course! I'm sorry," he said with a grin. "I was just mesmerized by the beauty of the graphs."

Autumn gestured to the screen. "But I haven't even gotten to the data portion of the presentation yet."

Isaac held up his hands. "Okay. You busted me. I was mesmerized by the beauty of you."

She stared at her lap and Isaac saw a crease of a smile.

"We're supposed to be working on the presentation, remember?"

Isaac twisted in his chair and she looked up. "I haven't forgotten."

He placed two fingers under her chin and gently lifted. "But this is more fun. Tell me something. Why did you agree to come to the art museum with me?"

"That's easy. Their collection is unparalleled and my tour guide was utterly charming."

"Even though I don't know a thing about art?"

Autumn nodded and they burst out laughing.

"Wow, since you have so much confidence in me, I have some other things I'd like to show you."

Autumn cocked her head to one side. "Right now?"

Isaac stood up and, with his foot, pushed his chair against the wall. He took her hand and quickly pulled her to her feet.

"Yes, right now."

Without letting her hand go, he slid past her and sat down in her leather office chair.

"Hey!" Autumn exclaimed in protest and leaned against the desk.

He uttered a mock sigh of satisfaction. "This is much more comfortable than that old wooden thing." He looked from side to side and frowned. "But there's no place to put my arms."

Suddenly he pulled her into his lap, hardening instantly at the feel of her soft buttocks on his thighs.

"There. That's better. Sitting next to you was too tempting."

He wrapped his arms around her and pulled her even closer.

She trembled and exclaimed, "But what about the Witterman presentation?"

"It's not going anyplace," he soothed with a kiss on the tip of her nose. "But right now, you belong here. Where I can do this..."

Gently, he tucked a few curls over her right ear and kissed her earlobe.

"And this..." Isaac moved his lips along her jawline.

"Autumn, I want us to be as close as we can get for now."

He molded his hands around her waist and slowly moved them up her back. "Because now is all we have."

Isaac nuzzled her neck and the sound of her moan tickled his lips. "I just want to feel you."

He quickly unbuttoned her silk blouse and eased it down over her shoulders. "You're so beautiful," he whispered low. He stroked his fingers over the fabric of her bra, then traced his finger along her exposed skin.

"How'd you know I wear briefs?"

"Lucky guess?"

Her voice caught in her throat as he began to massage her breasts.

Isaac looked up and flashed her a devilish grin. "You wanna find out for real?"

Autumn straddled him firmly and then reached back and unclasped her bra. "Does this answer your question?"

As she slowly slid each strap from her shoulder, Isaac

hitched in a breath. The fire in her eyes and the sound of her bra hitting the floor only magnified his desire.

His eyes dipped down to her breasts, which seemed even larger and more luscious than he remembered them. Before he knew what he was doing, he reached out and cupped her heavy flesh in his hand, flicking one nipple gently until it stiffened at his touch.

Isaac placed his hands underneath her skirt and lifted her bottom slightly to move her even closer. He wanted to feel the heat between her legs and he wanted her to feel him getting harder and hotter.

Autumn sighed and her eyes slid shut. "More," she uttered through parted lips. "Please, Isaac."

Isaac swiveled the chair around so her back was against the edge of the desk. He gripped her waist and his mouth watered in anticipation as she clutched his head and slowly guided him toward heaven.

Felicia locked her office and shouldered her purse, glad to finally be heading home. Most days she was counting the minutes till five o'clock. But she had two new hires with paperwork that needed to be processed and that took time.

It wasn't like she had anyone at home waiting for her, she thought bitterly. While she was very attractive, she refused to date because the only man she wanted was Isaac. Trouble was, he didn't want her.

And for that, he would pay.

Since she was a little girl, her father had always taught her that she could have whatever she wanted, whenever she wanted it. Most of the time, she didn't have to work for what she wanted.

Sterling had given her this job, and even though she hated it, she stuck with it because it was easy and she got paid enough to buy everything her father wouldn't outright give her.

The only thing he couldn't give her was Isaac. They had nothing in common except the pursuit of money, but from the moment she met him, she was obsessed. She almost went so far as to install a hidden camera in his office, but she was afraid Sterling would somehow find out. So she was forced to keep her attraction to Isaac a secret, especially since at Paxton relationships between coworkers were strongly discouraged.

Perhaps her desire for Isaac was because she was white and he was black. Or maybe it stemmed from the need to pursue something she knew deep down she'd always wanted but would never have. Like her father's love.

Unlike her, Isaac couldn't be bought. He couldn't even be seduced. She'd tried and failed miserably.

But he could be fired.

And when that day occurred, Isaac would finally realize that he needed her because she was the critical link to Sterling. He would come to her, on his knees, begging for his job back, and she would make damn sure that their first meeting would occur in her bedroom.

Felicia walked down the hall to the elevator, idly thinking about calling a friend for dinner so she wouldn't have to eat alone again.

She checked her watch, squinting at the dial. It was

after six o'clock and, on orders of her father, many of the overhead lights were automatically dimmed to save money on electricity. Sterling wanted less of Paxton's profits in the hands of Con Edison and more in his pockets. Plus, going green and reducing Paxton's corporate footprint was a smart business and public relations move.

As she walked past the last hallway before the elevator, she noticed a small wedge of light in front of Autumn's door and stopped in her tracks. According to the security tapes, Autumn had already developed a habit of leaving around four-thirty, which was totally ballsy considering the Paxton work day ended at five o'clock. That was another reason Felicia didn't like her and she was happy to make note of Autumn's leave time in her personnel file.

Isaac normally left around five-thirty, although he used to stay much later. Still, it worked in her favor, as she regularly snooped around in his office and those of other employees. She had keys to every room and every office at Paxton. It always amazed her the types of things people would keep in their desks, naively assuming no one else would ever discover them, or use it against them.

Felicia started down the corridor, for once grateful for the carpeting that her father had installed years prior. It was ugly but it sure came in handy for sneaking around.

As she approached, she didn't hear a sound but looked behind her once just to be sure she was alone.

She stopped short of Autumn's office door and took a deep breath before peeking through the little window.

At the sight of Isaac's lean muscular body folded over Autumn's exposed skin, her eyes widened. When Autumn arched away from the ugly metal desk, Felicia clenched her fists into a ball.

Isaac's hand slowly caressed Autumn's abdomen and Felicia felt her knees weaken. But like a tree with roots gnarled into the ground, she stood firm and watched the scene unfold as if she were in a trance.

Not wanting to see, but not having the strength to tear her eyes away from the sight of Isaac's bent head, she watched his large hands knead Autumn's skin and his full mouth roam everywhere it could reach. Lips she had so desperately wanted on her own body were now hungrily seeking and sucking—someone else.

In that moment, the lust she felt for Isaac was instantly replaced with a deep hatred that seeped through her veins like a sieve.

Fingers raked Isaac's bare back, and limbs Felicia wished she could snap in two hugged his trim waist, when through the thunder roaring in her ears and the jealousy burning in her heart, there suddenly came the muffled cries of a woman in love.

Chapter 12

Autumn tapped her foot on the marble floor of the apartment lobby. If Isaac didn't hurry, they were going to be late for the meeting with Ms. Witterman.

But in reality, punctuality was the least of her problems.

The doorman winked at her as if he could read her thoughts and she pasted a nervous smile on her face. She didn't know which was worse: keeping a secret or the desire to expose it to the world.

Or at least to the man you loved.

Autumn faced the mirrors that lined the walls and fiddled with the collar of her coat.

Love. Was that what she felt for Isaac? Or was she simply playing a role that would result in heartbreak for both of them?

Right now, all she was sure of was that she desired him more than she had any other man. Her need fueled her dreams and also stoked her fears.

More than anything, Autumn didn't want to hurt Isaac.

Knowing that her every thought, touch and kiss was hinged on a lie was getting to be more than she could bear. She was getting in too deep and it was time to step back. Loving Isaac was bad for her, worse for him and potentially disastrous for the case.

Being alone with him earlier in the week had made her come to her senses, and she knew she couldn't be alone with him like that again.

They'd almost made love that evening, right on the top of her desk, which was about as comfortable as that long-ago night when she'd camped in the desert and just as hot. The memory of his hands and tongue on her skin was so real that it made her blush, as if he were right there in front of her, covering the sounds of her climaxing with a kiss.

And when she had begged Isaac to go on, he'd told her it wasn't the right time and seemed content to pleasure her in his arms.

As it turned out, Isaac was right. Time was definitely not on her side, and the more time she spent with him, the deeper she would fall. So she started to edge away, or tried to at least.

For the rest of the week, Autumn insisted that they meet at a local coffee shop in the evenings to review the presentation, instead of in her office or apartment.

Isaac protested at first, but eventually, they came to

a silent understanding and settled into a routine where they were able to focus on the task at hand.

They both knew the importance of this deal.

If all went well today, Autumn would be able to present her findings to Sterling on Monday and that evening be on a plane to her next case.

After extensive research, she had found no evidence of any wrongdoing on Isaac's part, which was great, but it didn't make leaving him any easier.

At the sound of the elevator bell, Autumn checked her appearance in the mirror. She could hear Devon and Deshauna arguing even before the door opened. The two were still going at it when they walked out, with Isaac following close behind.

"I told you not to go into my backpack," Deshauna hollered.

Devon shrugged. "I needed a pencil. How was I supposed to know you kept your diary in there?" He turned to Isaac. "Do you think she really kissed James?"

Deshauna gasped in horror and dropped her backpack to the floor. "That's my private business." She lunged for her brother. "I'm gonna knock your—"

"Whoa! Hold on," Isaac commanded, stepping in between the two just in time. "Nobody's kissing or knocking anything. We'll talk about this tonight. Now you guys better get to school before you're late."

Devon made a quick getaway while Deshauna picked up her bag, her brow still furrowed in anger.

She started to head for the door but stopped when Isaac put his arm around her shoulder.

"I'm sorry that happened. Boys are stupid sometimes. Trust me, I know." He gave her a gentle hug. "Your secret is safe with me."

Deshauna smiled shyly. "Thanks, Dad." She broke away from his embrace. "See you later."

When she was gone, Isaac turned on his heel and walked the short distance to where Autumn stood waiting.

She smiled. "You really handled that well."

Isaac set down his briefcase and buttoned his coat. "Thanks. But I've still got a lot to learn about teenagers, sibling rivalry and first kisses."

"Well, at least you've got the kissing thing down pat," Autumn blurted out, immediately regretting voicing her observations.

"I do, huh?" Isaac replied with a sexy smile. "Care to try again and make sure?"

Autumn hitched in a breath as he wrapped one arm around her waist and pulled her to him. "I didn't get a chance to run this morning and I need something to wake me up."

"But you run every morning. What happened?"

He dropped his arm from around her waist. "I don't recall telling you that. How did you know?"

"I—uh," she stammered as the doorman went outside to flag down a cab. She pointed at him. "He did."

At that was partly true.

There was no point in mentioning the money she paid the man for that initial tidbit of information and for calling her every morning when Isaac left for his run, so that she could get out of the building before he came back. Now that Isaac knew she lived in the building, her money stayed in her wallet where it belonged.

Isaac placed his hands on his hips and stared at the doorman. "Billy? So much for privacy. I think it's time for a little talk."

Autumn reached for his arm as he started off. The case was almost complete. She didn't need Billy blowing her cover and ruining everything.

"No, it's time for us to leave for the presentation. The man made a little mistake. Let it go."

Isaac looked toward the door and then back at her. "You're right. He's a good guy."

Billy strode in their direction. "Cab this morning, sir?"

Isaac nodded and picked up his briefcase. Billy held the door and whistled for a taxi at the same time. Seconds later, one arrived and they got in. Their backs pressed against the seat as the taxi suddenly lurched away from the curb.

Autumn shivered and rubbed her gloved hands together. "Another cold morning in New York," she complained.

"I can't control the weather," Isaac replied, as he put his left arm around her. "But I know something that will warm you up."

He reached around and caressed her cheek with the palm of his right hand, the semi-rough texture heightening every stroke upon her soft skin. She leaned into his embrace and lifted her chin.

Isaac traced the shape of her lips with the tip of his finger. Her insides quaked at the tender gesture and she leaned into his embrace, forgetting that she wasn't supposed to want more.

"You're really special to me. Do you know that?"

She gulped in surprise at his words. "No," she admitted. He lifted her chin, forcing her to look in his eyes. "Then let me show you."

Isaac's lips trailed slowly over hers, one corner to the other, as if discovering their taste, so gently that he nearly brought her to tears. She reached up and grasped the back of his neck and pulled him closer, opening her mouth to accept his tongue.

Autumn kissed him back with a fervor that would later on astonish her. But, for right now, everything blurred and nothing mattered except for the moment they were creating together.

He groaned as he probed the inside of her mouth, his lips grinding against hers. With every kiss, their passion increased and so did the desperation to capture and hold on to it, each knowing that it had to end.

Still, they held the kiss and each other as the taxi raced over bumpy roads and swerved through honking traffic, each not caring about the final destination.

The taxi stopped suddenly, breaking their embrace and bringing them both back to reality.

Isaac exhaled deeply and grinned. "With a kiss like that, I'll never have to drink coffee again."

Autumn nodded distractedly and barely heard his statement. She was worried that Sterling was in the lobby, waiting for them. If he had seen them kissing, she knew he wouldn't be happy, plus it would destroy any trust he had in her to conduct an impartial investigation.

She grabbed her purse and quickly exited the taxi. She smiled at the doorman, who already had the lobby door open for her, and she was relieved that Sterling was nowhere in sight.

Isaac caught up and reached for her hand, but she took a few steps back, avoiding his touch.

He gave her a strange look. "Are you okay?"

She briefly touched her lips, still burning from his kisses, and nodded.

"Yes, I just want to get this presentation over with, know what I mean?"

Before she could walk away, he ran his hand slowly down her arm, the heat of his palm somehow searing through the heavy fabric of her wool coat, and she felt her knees weaken.

Isaac took a step and closed the gap between them. "And when it's all over, what are we going to do then?"

His voice was low and her loins tightened at his question, a hidden promise of continued passion.

"I guess we'll have to wait and find out."

But Autumn already knew the answer. She was leaving Isaac forever.

Isaac examined Autumn's face as they rode the private elevator to Eleanor Witterman's penthouse apartment.

She seemed to want to be with him, but the abrupt change in her demeanor led him to believe she was holding something back, too. The passion for him was assuredly there. He felt it in her kiss, heard it in her cries when he'd pleasured her to orgasm in her office, and that memorable first time in her apartment.

Still, there was an inexplicable hesitation on Autumn's part and before they moved to the next level in their relationship, Isaac knew he had to put her at ease somehow.

He had to tell her his feelings about her even though he was still trying to figure them out himself. It wouldn't be easy, for he realized he wasn't a very outwardly emotional man. But inside, the intense feelings she invoked in him were raw, powerful and very scary.

The elevator doors opened and Sterling greeted them.

"Here they are, Eleanor. We were wondering what happened to you both."

Isaac and Autumn stepped out onto the marbled floor.

"We left in plenty of time, but crosstown traffic was a mess this morning," he lied.

A tall woman with a regal air walked toward them, holding a small dog in her arms.

"Not to worry, dears. Sterling and I have been having a grand time catching up on old times. Haven't we?"

"Old times?" Autumn asked in a confused voice.

Sterling appeared embarrassed. He put his hands behind his back and cleared his throat. "Eleanor and I are old friends, and I'm hoping that after today, I'll be able to call her a client, too," he said tersely.

The latter statement was obviously directed at Isaac and Autumn and was followed by a yip from the dog.

"We'll do our best," Autumn replied hastily, cutting her eyes at the bundle of fur.

"I'm eager to hear where you think I should invest some of my money. It was a good thing Sterling called me when he did," she added. "I was ready to leave it all to my little Pookie."

When Ms. Witterman pursed her lips and started making obnoxious kissing noises at the little fur ball, Isaac glanced over at Autumn, who appeared to be struggling not to laugh.

"What do you say we get started then?"

"Great idea," Sterling replied hastily. "We're going to be meeting in the media room. Eleanor, will you direct us?"

She nodded and set Pookie down on the floor, and they all followed her to a room on the farthest edge of the luxurious penthouse. When she opened the door and Isaac took one look at the movie-theater-like setting, complete with a popcorn machine on wheels, he knew he had to have a similar room in his own apartment.

"This is fantastic," Isaac commented, setting his briefcase on the floor. "It would be great for watching sports or movies with my k—" He stopped himself just before saying the word *kids*. "I mean friends."

But thankfully, Sterling and Eleanor weren't even listening. They were busy getting Pookie settled. Apparently the dog had his own booster seat.

He turned to Autumn, shaken inside at his near error. Now wasn't the time to reveal to Sterling the fact that he had two children and the reasons he chose to keep them a secret.

"That was close," he whispered, shrugging out of his coat and laying it over a nearby seat.

She unzipped her laptop bag and nodded. "I know."

She squeezed his hand, her touch instantly calming him.

Autumn handed him the laptop. "Let's get the computer set up. The sooner we get this over with, the better."

Isaac kept his eyes on hers as she took off her coat, hoping she could see the grateful look in his eyes.

Turning away, he located an elaborate console in a small closet. In just a few minutes, he was able to figure out how to get the presentation to display on the large plasma screen.

When Isaac joined Autumn in front of the room, Sterling and Eleanor were already sitting in the second row, with Pookie in the seat between them happily gnawing on a small bone.

He dug his small laser pointer out of the inside of his suit coat, smiled at Autumn and then at the group in front of him.

"Ms. Witterman, thank you for having us here today. Autumn and I are excited to represent Paxton Investment Securities to discuss our plan to grow your capital through a sound investment strategy that we predict will result in long-lasting and profitable dividends."

"Show me the money!" replied Eleanor enthusiastically, backed by Pookie, who looked up from her bone and yipped in agreement.

Three hours later, Isaac and Autumn emerged from Eleanor Witterman's penthouse apartment exhausted and unsure.

While their potential client had listened intently and had asked a ton of questions, which they and Sterling had taken turns patiently answering, neither knew if she was on board.

"She really had her poker face on," remarked Isaac. "I think that was one of the most stressful presentations in my entire career."

"It was pretty nerve-racking," Autumn agreed as she slipped her arms into her coat. "But that damn Pookie dog sure made out like a bandit. Did you see how many biscuits Witterman fed him?"

"Yeah," Isaac agreed, laughing heartily. "I think he wanted us to convince her to invest in the pet industry instead of diamonds, technology, health care and wind engineering."

Autumn cracked up and they were both laughing as they made their way to the lobby door.

"Isaac! Autumn! Wait!" Sterling called out.

They turned and watched as he strode quickly to them.

"I'm glad to see you're both in a good mood. I have news."

Sterling slapped Isaac on the back. "She loves the strategy you guys presented. Congratulations, we won!"

Isaac and Autumn turned to each other, wanting to embrace with joy but knowing they couldn't.

"That's wonderful," Autumn replied.

Isaac added, "Coming out of the meeting, we weren't sure. It was hard to gauge her reaction to our ideas."

Before Isaac could ask if Autumn would be involved, Sterling stuck out his hand. Isaac shook it, followed by Autumn.

"Great job, both of you. She'll be in our offices sometime on Monday to sign the contract. Isaac, be sure to clear your schedule."

Sterling checked his watch. "It's way past lunchtime, plus it's Friday. Why don't both of you take the rest of the day off. You deserve it."

"Thank you, sir," Isaac replied. "Are you headed back to the office now?"

Sterling shook his head and adjusted his tie. "I'm going to go back upstairs and try to convince Eleanor to go to lunch with me."

"Good luck," Autumn said.

Isaac and Autumn watched as Sterling hopped into the elevator and smoothed his hair. Just before the doors closed, he gave them the thumbs-up.

They walked outside, where a taxi sat idling and the long Friday afternoon stretched pleasantly before them. The sun was shining, making it seem warmer than it really was, and Isaac felt like a heavy load had been lifted from his shoulders.

Winning the Witterman pitch was the last hurdle to his becoming a partner at Paxton. Once that happened, he'd be able to tell Sterling about his kids and he would have achieved everything he'd ever wanted in life.

There was just one thing missing. The love of the woman standing before him.

Autumn looked back at the building and shook her head in amazement. "Now that was really strange. I don't think I've ever seen Sterling so happy. He's normally such a grump."

"Me neither," he responded, belatedly shrugging into

his coat. "And I don't think winning the deal had anything to do with it."

She turned back as he was picking up his briefcase and he smiled at the curious look on her face.

"What do you mean?" she asked.

His eyes floated slowly over her beautiful face, the lithe body that, ever since he'd met her, he craved night and day.

"Let's go home and I'll show you."

Isaac reached for her hand and his heart lifted in his chest when, this time, she took it willingly.

Chapter 13

The cab eased away from the curb and Autumn knew there was no going back.

Her bare hand, still firmly clasped in Isaac's, and the utter calm she felt in the depths of her spirit, were both proof that she was about to risk everything for what lay ahead.

The silence between them gave her time to think, and she idly wondered if she was being foolish or, worse, naive. But Autumn forced those thoughts from her mind. If she had to, she would admit to being a lot of things.

Ambitious.

Willful.

Defiant when she had to be. Harsh, too, although the barbs she dealt were primarily directed at herself.

Some people would call these personality flaws; she preferred to think of them as her protection. Her dad had taught her to never let her guard down, for right around the corner, waiting in the dark and ready to leap, was the unknown.

Thus, naïveté didn't fall into the realm of her existence. Her new life as a private investigator was far too unpredictable for her to be anything but completely confident in her decisions.

She looked out the window and squeezed Isaac's hand. A tense and palpable excitement hung in the air around them, waiting to be unwrapped and explored. In her mind, she cursed the lumbering midday traffic and urged the taxi to drive faster..

When they finally arrived, they hopped out and Isaac suddenly turned and pulled her aside, and she almost slipped on a patch of ice.

She opened her mouth to protest, but he leaned his cheek against hers, his breath hot in her ears. "I want to make love to you, Autumn."

Isaac's voice was low and urgent. "Really make love to you."

He caressed her earlobe with the edge of his mouth and she shivered against his overcoat. "And I don't want you to say anything. Just follow my lead, okay?"

Autumn knew it was crazy, to be at this man's bidding. But, without a moment's hesitation, she found herself nodding her head.

Some would call her decision selfish, since she was leaving town in a few days. But she didn't think it was wrong to take one afternoon of passion with her. Memories were the only things that lasted anyway. Relationships sure didn't. They only got in the way of, well, everything.

This was the right decision, for it would protect both of them from eventual and mutual heartbreak.

Isaac draped his arm around her shoulder and they walked inside the building. As they rode the private elevator up to his penthouse, he pressed his body against hers and kissed her gently.

The doors opened and he backed her into the foyer, his lips never leaving her mouth.

She dropped her purse and he let go of his briefcase, not caring at the moment if the laptops and cell phones within suffered any damage when they hit the marble floor. Their only concern was the inner world of pleasure they were in the midst of creating for themselves.

Autumn's hands drifted up Isaac's back, the heavy fabric of his coat tickling her palms, while he got busy unbuttoning her coat. He eased it over her shoulders and she shivered and broke out in goose bumps in spite of the heat between them.

"Cold?" he asked, shedding his own coat.

She nodded, feeling as needy as a child yet wanting him like a woman.

"I know just the thing that will warm you up."

He led her to the master bathroom and started the water in the huge Jacuzzi tub.

She stepped out of her shoes, trembling in anticipation. As the water ran, he quickly undressed her. She thought it was odd that he did not caress her skin and she found herself yearning for his touch.

When he began to undress, she started to turn away, her nipples puckering painfully in the cool air.

"Watch me," he commanded.

She felt his eyes on her face as he undid his belt and his trousers fell to the tile floor, revealing the bulge of his erection, the outline so deliciously apparent in his white briefs that she bit her lip and prayed he removed his underwear next.

She let out a low groan of frustration when, instead, he slowly unknotted and removed his tie, and then his blue oxford shirt to reveal a muscular frame that seemed even more imposing and sexy in broad daylight.

Finally, Isaac slid his briefs down over his thighs and she gasped as the length of his penis sprang forth.

He placed one hand and ran it up and down the shaft. "Do you like what you see in front of you?"

She pursed her lips and nodded in response.

"So do I. You're beautiful, Autumn. Do you know that?"

It was a good thing he'd commanded her not to speak, for she didn't know how to answer his question. She never thought of herself as beautiful. Pretty, maybe, but never beautiful.

Autumn held her breath as Isaac went to her, his penis jutting out between them, and cupped her face in his hands.

"If you don't think you're beautiful, you will soon," he said urgently.

After grabbing a couple of towels, he turned off the water, took her hand and helped her step into the tub.

"Wait," he said, stepping in after her. "Before you sit down, there's something I need to do. Turn around with your back to me."

Autumn did so and when Isaac traced his finger down the hollow of her spine, from her neck to the crest of her ass, she began to shudder uncontrollably and put her palms against the wall to steady herself.

He ridged a finger against the soft folders of her outer lips and the intense rush of pleasure she experienced as he slid it back and forth made her hands curl into fists.

Isaac sucked in a low breath. "Already wet. Good." He pulled her up against him, and she felt his hard penis roll against the small of her back. "I knew you wanted me."

He wrested her gently around to face him. And she saw that his eyes were as dark and as wanton as his actions.

I do! she wanted to cry out as they sank on their knees into the warm water. Her unsaid thoughts were quickly forgotten by the pressure of his mouth against hers, while their tongues entangled in a lush firestorm of intense need.

Their kiss seemed to last forever, and when Isaac broke away, she whimpered a little and reached for him again. He placed a finger upon her lips to shush her and she stuck her tongue out and licked it in defiance, enjoying his wide-eyed look of surprise.

Autumn gladly complied when Isaac motioned for

her to sit astride his lap, facing him. When her buttocks touched his hard thighs, he moaned and clutched each cheek in his hands, drawing her even closer.

She wrapped her legs around his waist and she didn't have to look down to see just how much Isaac wanted her. The evidence was pressed against her abdomen, taunting her. It took all her strength and will to not lift her hips and slowly guide him inside her.

Instead, she closed her eyes, leaned in and nuzzled at his neck. Inhaling Isaac's dense, spicy-musk scent made her feel more alive than she had in a long time. The slightly rough texture of sponge he used to gently wash her back and arms only added to the pleasant sensations. She couldn't remember the last time she'd felt so cared for by a man.

When he was finished, Isaac cupped her shoulder blades and leaned forward so her back was submerged in the water, washing the soap away. Without thinking, she tilted her head back, dampening her hair, and unwittingly exposed her breasts to the air.

His tongue flicked at one of her nipples and she yelped, and then moaned when he did it again. And again.

Isaac cupped and lifted her flesh in his hands. "Your breasts are so—"

He never finished as she held on to his head, keeping her abdomen tight so she wouldn't fall back into the water, while his tongue curled around each stiff tip, never yielding, never lifting. So warm and wet and steamy.

Finally, he broke away and caught her bottom lip in his teeth. "Let's get out of here."

Isaac exited the tub first and wrapped a towel around his waist. He smiled when her eyes locked on his torso where the fabric wasn't smooth.

When she managed to stand, she found that her legs were rubbery and she almost fell down. But Isaac grabbed her hand, wrapped her in a towel and swooped her into his arms.

The bedroom was only a few feet away and Isaac laid her on his enormous bed before slipping away to draw the curtains shut. He lit two candles on the dresser before returning to her side.

Isaac unwrapped her body from the towel and drew in a breath. She closed her eyes while he stood over her and rubbed her dry with the towel.

When he was finished, Autumn turned on her side and balanced her head on one elbow. His eyes were questioning when she reached out her finger and crooked it between the towel and his waist. With a just quick snap of her wrist, the towel was on the floor and his shaft was throbbing before her. She sat up and slipped him into her mouth, almost to the full hilt of his length, still moist from the bath.

He tilted his hips and groaned as she savored his length with her tongue, enjoying the thick fullness of his skin in her mouth, so velvety soft yet so virile. Capable of creating life and giving pleasure.

His groans became more guttural and he wove his hands through her curls as she sucked hard on the core of his strength. Teasing and taunting him to release, to expend the power he had over her, which she was now controlling with such acute mastery.

Finally, he clasped her cheeks in his palms, breathing heavily and she released him. Smiling, she fell back on the bed and stretched her arms over her head. Without a word, he slipped his hand under the small of her back and clutched at her waist, moving her farther up on the bed. The weight of his body upon hers made her yearn even more to be connected to him.

"Autumn, you drive me crazy enough to tell you that I think I'm falling in love with you."

She opened her mouth, dumbfounded at his confession and was just about to speak when he covered her lips with his own.

Edging her legs apart with his knee, he broke away and whispered in her ear. "Now just let me show you how much I love you."

Autumn gasped as he slid inside her easily and she wrapped her arms around his torso while he rocked his hips and her entire world.

Back and forth they moved together, the bedspread rippling underneath and around them. Isaac nipped at her breast, and her arm muscles tightened as she clenched the little dunes of fabric. She discovered that holding on only intensified the sweet agony, so she held on tighter.

Autumn lifted her head from the bed, hair matted against her neck. "Isaac! Oh, God. Please. Don't. Stop."

She folded her knees to her chest, inviting him to

plunge deeper. He did and, within moments, dove deeper still. The heavy weight of his testicles slapped between her thighs and against her moist outer lips until she thought she'd go mad.

As Isaac increased his pace, so did the fierce whirlwind of emotions that surrounded them, until release poured forth from a cloud of ecstasy.

Eyes wide open, hearts on fire, time forgotten.

Chapter 14

Autumn plopped down on her sofa, limbs extended like a scarecrow, and rubbed her eyes. She had read once somewhere that Sundays were either a time for reflection or regret. Today, she'd experienced plenty of both.

Her eyes welled with tears, still overwhelmed at Isaac's admission of love. Part of her wished his words were only a result of the heat of the moment. The other part prayed they were true.

He'd told her before she left on Friday that he was taking his children on their first ski trip. So, other than a few text messages, she hadn't been in contact with him all weekend. Maybe that was a good thing. He would get used to her not being around and she would get used to missing him terribly.

Autumn wiped the rag in her hand across her forehead, not caring at the moment that it was full of dust, and gazed out the window. It was already dark, the oppressive blue-black wintery hue that made her gloomy mood seem all the more real and her present situation downright inescapable.

Was this how a woman in love was supposed to feel?

Autumn didn't think so. Nor did she think she could face Isaac again, not when she'd betrayed him.

He didn't know that yet, but that's what she did.

Tomorrow morning, she was going to walk into Sterling's office with the final report of her investigation. As far as she could surmise, Isaac was innocent. And now that she knew him and loved him, she realized that there was nothing else he could be but completely free of wrongdoing.

She was the only one who had committed a crime whose only sentence was a broken heart for both of them.

Autumn straightened and leaned over to dust the coffee table. She saw her reflection in the glossy surface and wondered how she was going to explain to Isaac that she was leaving New York in two days.

To tell him the truth, she'd have to reveal the reason she was hired at Paxton in the first place.

To spy, to lie and to betray.

Not to love and then to leave.

But that's exactly what she planned to do.

Autumn moved her bare feet against the edge of the couch and felt something hard.

She slid to the floor and saw her favorite slipper, which had been missing for over a week.

"So that's where you've been!" she scolded, wedging her hand underneath the sofa to retrieve it. And with it came a set of papers, stapled together, that she hadn't known were there.

Autumn backed up against the sofa and sat cross-legged on the floor. The paper was a detailed report of a recent investment transaction conducted by Isaac for one of his clients. It was dated six months earlier, and attached was a copy of the check the client had given as payment. After flipping back and forth through the pages, she could not find any record that the client's payment was applied to Paxton's account.

She threaded one hand through her hair. She'd reviewed hundreds of similar documents for the past two weeks, and somehow she'd missed this one. It must have slipped under the couch on one of the many nights she'd fallen asleep there.

No big deal, she thought as she stood and walked into the kitchen. She would simply follow the same process she'd used with all of the previous reports and check it against the Paxton's accounting system.

She sat down and quickly logged into the Paxton financial network, yet after a few minutes of searching, she could find no record of the transaction.

With a ball quickly forming in the pit of her stomach, she logged out of the Paxton network and logged in to Isaac's personal bank accounts. After an advanced search, she discovered the exact amount of the client's check appeared as a deposit in one of Isaac's accounts.

Autumn's heart sank and she banged a fist on the table, wishing she'd never found the missing document. How could he have done it, she thought. How could he have stolen all that money?

No matter how she felt about Isaac, keeping this information to herself wasn't an option. She had to tell Sterling.

Autumn thought about calling him right away, but she'd already emailed him earlier that she had good news. There was no use in spoiling the man's evening when she could ruin his Monday morning.

She calmly packed up her laptop and slid the report into her bag. Her phone buzzed and her pulse quickened when she saw it was a text from Isaac. She slid her thumb over the top to read his message.

Back home. Missed you. Still cold from skiing.
Can I stop by so you can warm me up?

Autumn stared at the letters for a while before she turned off the lights in the rest of the apartment and headed to the bedroom. It was only when she'd gotten under the covers that she deleted Isaac's text and cried herself to sleep.

The next morning, Autumn left early to avoid running into Isaac and had breakfast at a diner. The pancakes were delicious, but so large that she knew she'd be in a carb coma before ten o'clock. She was on her second cup of tea by the time she arrived at Paxton and she went directly to Sterling's office.

His door was open, but she rapped on it anyway.

Sterling looked up, his brows knit together in a way that made him look instantly angry.

"Looks like the yen is going to ruin my Monday again," he muttered irritably.

"At least the Dow closed on an upswing last week," she offered. "And we closed the Witterman deal."

Sterling looked thoughtful, and then sighed. "Sometimes I wonder why I got into this business."

"To make money?" she offered, wishing he would stop waxing philosophical so she could tell him the bad news.

"No, Autumn. To change lives. Money can do that, you know," he instructed with a wan smile.

"It can also ruin lives," Autumn replied, pulling out the report she'd found last night.

"What's this?" Sterling asked, putting on his reading glasses.

"This is a report from approximately six months ago, a client by the name of Ginsaro."

Sterling reached for the report and she handed it to him.

"Yes, what about it?" he asked impatiently.

"I discovered client funds were never entered into the Paxton financial system. Instead they were deposited into Isaac's personal checking account the same day."

Sterling laid the paper on his desk and glared at her.

"In your email last night, you indicated that your investigation was complete and that you found no potentially criminal evidence."

Autumn nodded. "At the time, that was correct. But

late last night, I discovered this document underneath my couch, and then I logged on to the network and—"

He waved his hand, cutting her off. "Are you sure about all this?"

"I wish I could say no, but I can't."

Sterling nodded grimly and picked up his phone. He stabbed at the buttons. "Felicia, get in here," he barked.

Autumn's stomach clenched. If Felicia was being called into the meeting, that could only mean one thing.

She approached his desk and hoped she wouldn't sound like she was begging. "I think you should give Isaac a chance to explain. There must be a reason or perhaps a misunderstanding."

Sterling raised an eyebrow. "Don't worry, Autumn. We have procedures in place to deal with these kinds of situations." He checked his watch. "He should be here any minute. If you recall, we were scheduled to talk at nine-thirty about finalizing the Witterman deal. Eleanor will be here just before noon to sign all the paperwork, which in light of your discovery, I will now personally handle instead of Isaac."

Felicia stalked into the room without knocking and without acknowledging Autumn.

One of the perks of being the boss's daughter, Autumn thought.

She tossed her blond hair over her shoulder. "What's going on, Daddy? I'm in the middle of something important."

"I need you in here for a meeting that I'm having with Isaac in just a few minutes."

Felicia cocked a brow and stared at Autumn. "Isaac?

I just saw him running down the hall to his office. Do you want me to go get him?"

"No need," Sterling replied. "I'm sure he'll be here soon. You two might as well sit down and wait."

Both women settled down into chairs at a small conference table that was located diagonally from Sterling's desk. Autumn wished she could stare at the buildings outside rather than at the door, but her back was to the windows.

There was a tense silence in the room, as they waited for Isaac. No one bothered to make small talk.

Through the corner of her eye, Autumn caught a glimpse of Felicia, who was watching her intently. More than anything, Autumn wished she could wipe the smug look off her face. The witch knew something. It was almost as if she was expecting trouble and was getting ready to enjoy it.

When Isaac arrived, Autumn drew in a sharp breath.

"Good morning, Sterling. How was your weekend?" he said cheerfully, walking in.

From the doorway, the two women weren't visible, but as Isaac approached Sterling's desk, he turned his head.

Autumn's heart beat faster as he caught her eye and nodded, his eyes lighting up in a way that was only meant for her.

The memory of those same eyes squeezed shut as he kept pace with the urgent rhythm of his lovemaking scraped through Autumn's mind and her body warmed at its most intimate core.

"I'm sorry, I didn't see you ladies there. What is this? A party?" he joked.

"I'm afraid not," Sterling replied, his tone anything but funny. "Please sit down."

Isaac edged a quick glance at Autumn. Somehow she was able to keep her face unchanged, although inside she wanted to scream. At herself mostly, because she was powerless to warn him about what was going to happen next.

He sat and crossed one leg over a knee. "Sure, what's going on?"

Sterling pulled his chair closer to the desk and folded his hands. "It has come to my attention that some client funds are missing from the Paxton accounts. The money was deposited into a personal bank account, instead of ours."

Isaac looked confused. "So, what's that got to do with me?"

Sterling glared at him. "The client is yours and so is the bank account."

Isaac slowly put his foot on the floor. "What are you talking about? What client?" he asked, leaning forward.

"Dr. Ginsaro," Sterling replied.

"But he passed away months ago. I've been trying to get in touch with the lawyer handling his estate, but no luck."

"That's a very convenient excuse," Sterling snapped. "A game of phone tag doesn't explain how $100,000 ended up in your bank account and not ours."

"But I don't know what you're talking about!" Isaac

insisted, raising his voice. "I've never even seen the check."

"First of all, watch your tone. Second of all, as of right now, you are suspended without pay, pending further investigation of these allegations."

"B-but, I didn't do anything wrong!" Isaac sputtered.

"Felicia!" Sterling said, ignoring Isaac. "Call custodial services and get Isaac a box so he can take his personal items with him. You have thirty minutes to leave the premises."

Isaac leaned forward in his chair, looking as though he wanted to throttle Sterling's neck.

"But this is bull! What evidence do you have?"

"We have certain documentation, which will be shared with you upon approval of our counsel. May I suggest you retain your own attorney?"

"I'm not going anywhere. I didn't do anything!" he raged.

His eyes caught Autumn's again, and this time they were frantic. She shook her head, almost imperceptibly, hoping he would avoid further trouble and just go. Although she yearned to speak up and defend him, she couldn't deny what she'd found, any more than she could deny her feelings for him.

Felicia got up and walked over to Sterling's side. "Don't make me call security," she warned.

Isaac flattened his palms on his thighs and stood abruptly. With his chin high, he stalked out of the room.

Felicia followed him to the door and Autumn heard her mutter "Good riddance" under her breath as she shut the door. She sat in the chair Isaac had just vacated.

"Do you want me to prepare the termination papers?"

Sterling didn't glance up from his computer, where he was already typing away as if nothing had happened. "Hold off until I tell you to move forward."

Felicia folded her arms and huffed. "But why? We have everything we need to fire him."

Sterling stopped typing and stared at his daughter as if he was seeing her for the first time. "Not quite. Hold off. End of discussion."

"Well, at least tell me why Autumn is here. For legal purposes, we have rules around who is supposed to be present in the room when someone is reprimanded or terminated. Only you and I should have been in this meeting."

"Autumn is here because she *is* the law," Sterling responded grimly.

Felicia turned around and Autumn enjoyed the look of shock on her face. "You're a cop?"

"No, I'm a private investigator under contract with the U.S. government, to investigate suspected cases of corporate fraud."

She faced Sterling. "Daddy, how did you know?"

"I had some suspicions and I hired Autumn to look into things more carefully."

He stared at his daughter, and Autumn detected a hint of challenge in his eyes.

"I may be getting old, Felicia, but I'm still aware of everything that goes on, and goes wrong, in my company."

Yikes! Autumn thought, quickly planning her escape before she became embroiled in a father-daughter battle.

She stood up and put her coat on. "If you don't need anything else, I've got to get home and pack."

Sterling walked around his desk. "I appreciate everything you've done," he said, extending his hand.

Autumn nearly winced at his strong grip. "No problem at all."

"When are you leaving town?"

"I fly out late tomorrow evening for another case."

Sterling looked impressed. "The government must keep you pretty busy."

"There are plenty of greedy people out there."

Sterling laughed, unaware that her comment was directed toward him.

"Anyway, please feel free to call me if you need anything further," Autumn continued.

She turned to Felicia. "I believe I may have left one of my favorite scarves in my office. Under the circumstances, I don't think it's wise that I go and get it myself."

Sterling's face had a sober expression as he turned to his daughter. "Go check on Isaac and make sure he doesn't take his laptop with him. There's obviously a lot of data on there we don't want him to have access to for now."

He walked back to his desk and sat down. "Felicia will locate your scarf and mail it to you. Thanks again and good luck."

Autumn nodded and walked out of the room, heading in the opposite direction of her former office, for the stairwell. If Isaac was still here, she didn't want to risk running into him at the elevators. She was almost there when she felt a hand grasp her arm.

Before she even turned around, she knew who it was.

"Thanks for not ratting me out in front of my father."

Autumn shrugged. "He's the one paying the bill."

Felicia laughed softly. "Yes. Thank goodness." Her eyes narrowed. "I'll be sure to take good care of Isaac. He'll need someone to turn to now. Someone other than you."

"There's nothing between us, Felicia."

She raised a brow. "Oh no? Well, in that case, I trust you won't have a problem with me satisfying his needs on something other than some old desk."

Autumn felt her cheeks get hot with embarrassment.

"That's right, Autumn. I did a little spying of my own."

"You're sick," she spit out.

Felicia looked thoughtful. "Perhaps, but then again, I'm not the one who has to screw people to get information out of them."

Autumn turned her back, pulled open the door and started her way down the steps, irked that Felicia was right. Dishonesty was at the root of her undercover work. She'd lost count of all the nights she'd lain awake contemplating the irony.

Still, she loved what she did and couldn't fathom doing anything else, regardless of the duplicitous things she needed to do or say in order to get the job done.

Deep in her heart, though, she knew there was nothing false about her love for Isaac, her need to be close to him, but now there was nothing she could do to tell him the truth.

Like her true identity, she had to hide her feelings for Isaac to protect him, as well as herself.

Felicia stood at the door, frowning as she listened to Autumn's heels clanging down the metal stairwell. She was glad that Autumn was out of the way, but she didn't appreciate being played for a fool.

Neither would Isaac once he learned the truth.

She turned and set off for Isaac's office. Autumn was sneaky, conniving and now totally unable to defend herself. Felicia knew this was the right time to reapproach Isaac to lend her support.

When she arrived, Isaac was just locking his office.

"Did you leave your laptop in there?"

"I'm not even going to justify that question with a response."

She ignored his glare and held out her left hand. "I'll take those."

He dropped the keys into her cupped palm. "This is all a sham, Felicia."

She flashed an innocent smile and leaned one shoulder against the wall. "Even if that's true, and I'm not saying that it is, you're not the only one at Paxton who has been deceived."

"I highly doubt that," he retorted.

"We've both been played by the same woman."

His face contorted. "Who? What do you mean?"

"You'll never guess," Felicia said with a drawn-out smile, enjoying the discomfort in Isaac's eyes. "Autumn

Hilliard. She's a private detective, not an investment analyst, as you and I both originally thought."

"What kind of craziness are you peddling now, Felicia."

"It's true. My father hired her to investigate you. She's a fraud." Felicia shrugged, keeping her eyes pinned on his. "I guess that's one thing you both had in common."

His eyes widened in shock and he looked over at Autumn's office. "You're wrong!"

Felicia put her hand on her chest and adopted a solemn tone. "I wish I was. I feel horrible. I mean, if word gets out that I allowed a private investigator to be hired, even if it was by my father, the other departments at Paxton will lose trust in my abilities as a human resources professional."

Isaac shot her another glare. "It's always about you, isn't it?"

Felicia laughed and tossed her blond hair. "You're very astute." She stepped toward Isaac and ran a finger down the lapel of his coat. "But I'm more than happy to make this about you…and me."

"Cut it out, Felicia."

He pushed her hand away and her stomach clenched in anger.

"You know, you really should be nicer to me. After all, I didn't tell Sterling about your little tête-à-tête with Autumn in her office. In case you forgot, we have strict rules here at Paxton about public displays of affection."

"That didn't stop you, did it?"

She laughed again and wrapped her arms around his neck. "When I see something I want, I always get it."

He twisted away, breaking her hold. "I said, cut it out. I don't want you," he retorted in a disgusted tone. "I want—"

Isaac looked again at Autumn's closed door and Felicia enjoyed the pained expression on his face.

"What you want, Isaac…is a lie. Don't you see that?"

She felt vaguely satisfied when he didn't say another word and instead walked away.

He'll be back. I'll make sure of it.

There was nothing better than betrayal to cause a man to flee…right into another woman's arms.

Chapter 15

Isaac rubbed his eyes and yawned as he waited for his children in the kitchen. A cup of coffee, long since gone cold, was the only remnant of a sleepless night. Normally, he would have made an attempt at cooking breakfast, but not this morning when all he wished he could do was to talk to Autumn.

She hadn't responded to texts or phone calls, and when he knocked on her door last night, she didn't answer. To add to his frustration, the doorman wouldn't say if she'd returned to or left the building.

The woman he loved, and who he thought perhaps loved him, seemed to have disappeared into thin air. She was as elusive as the feelings they once shared.

Isaac leaned over the table and stared into the coffee cup, as if it would give him an answer to his biggest question.

He was innocent. Why would she investigate a sham?

All he wanted from her now was an explanation, and maybe a little help in clearing his name.

Isaac lifted his head and checked the time on the microwave. "Kids! Hurry up or you're going to be late for school," he said in a halfhearted yell.

Deshauna sauntered in, touching her hair to make sure her style was still intact. She hoisted her backpack over her shoulder and eyed the table. "I don't want cereal again this morning. Can I have some money to grab a bagel on my way to school?"

Isaac nodded. "There's a ten-dollar bill on my dresser. Don't spend it all at once."

"Thanks, Dad," she called back, already halfway to his room. "I'll see you later."

"Wait a minute. Aren't you going to wait for your brother?"

But his question fell on deaf ears because a moment later, he heard the door slam.

Isaac sighed. As much as he wanted Devon and Deshauna to stick together as before, the pair had become much more independent since the adoption. That was a wonderful thing, but it also meant that he had to worry more about them. New York City had a lot of tempting people, places and things for teenagers, and not all of it was good.

Devon ran into the room, jolting Isaac out of his thoughts.

"Hey, Dad." He stopped just before he got to the table. "Why are you still in your pajamas?"

He was glad at least one of his children had noticed that he wasn't in his normal attire for a Tuesday morning.

"I'm not feeling well this morning, son."

Devon glanced outside and shrugged. "Oh. I thought it was because we had a snow day."

"Sorry to disappoint you, bud, but snow days are pretty rare in NYC."

"I know, Dad, but I can still hope, can't I?"

Devon sat down and poured some cereal into a bowl. He was the only kid Isaac knew who ate cereal without milk.

"So what's wrong, Dad?"

His son's earnest tone made him thankful once again that he decided to adopt. Isaac rubbed at the stubble on his chin. "Well. Something that I thought would work out…didn't, so I guess I'm feeling a little down this morning."

He didn't bother mentioning the fact that, for the time being, he also no longer had a job.

"You know what, Dad? Before you adopted us, I was ready to give up." He finished munching on some cereal and swallowed before continuing.

"We'd been waiting so long for someone. But the evening before we all first met, I told myself that I wasn't going to quit hoping. And as soon as I started believing that in my heart, everything fell into place."

Devon looked around the room, as if he couldn't believe his good fortune. The brightness of his smile could have powered a small city.

"It works, Dad. You should try it!"

Isaac glanced around, but all he saw was expensive cabinetry and appliances he barely knew how to use.

He grinned wide, even though he didn't feel like it. "That's great advice, Devon."

"When I grow up, I want to be a good guy. Just like you."

Isaac felt the corners of his eyes smart, which happened whenever he felt like crying, but he held them back.

He reached over and patted his son's head. "Thanks, bud. I have no doubt you will."

Isaac leaned back and rubbed away the emotion from his eyes. "Better get going before you're late for school."

Devon nodded and jumped out of his chair. With a final wave goodbye, he ran down the hall and out the door.

Isaac slumped in his chair. He needed a fresh cup of coffee badly, but he didn't feel like making any; nor did he feel like getting dressed to go out and buy one.

A few minutes past nine, his phone rang. His heart raced as he reached for it and then fell in disappointment. It was Sterling.

"Good morning, Isaac. How are you?" Sterling bellowed.

"I've had better days," Isaac muttered, holding his phone away from his ear.

"I was wondering if you had lunch plans," Sterling continued, not missing a beat.

"Well, I was going to catch up on my favorite soap opera, but I just learned it was canceled three years ago, so I'm free," Isaac replied.

"Wonderful." Sterling gave him the name of a restaurant on the Upper East Side. "I'll see you at noon."

"What's this all about?" Isaac cut in, but Sterling had already ended the call. He stared at the phone for a second, wondering if he should call his lawyer, before sliding the device across the table in disgust.

Yesterday around this time, Sterling was busy accusing him of one of the worst crimes in business. Now twenty-four hours later he was inviting him to lunch?

Isaac rubbed the bridge of his nose trying to erase the memory of the compliment his son Devon had given him earlier. It was untrue and one that he didn't deserve. Would a good guy let the best job and the best woman he ever had in his life slip away?

With a resigned sigh, Isaac got up and walked down the hall to the bathroom for a shower. He might feel like a bum, but he didn't have to look like one.

Three hours later, Isaac and Sterling sat in a booth at Rudy's, an upscale sports bar and restaurant at 90th and York. The room was crowded with people trying to escape the workday grind if only for an hour, wishing it were three. Many were drinking beer.

Isaac looked around at the wide-screen televisions and neon liquor signs. "I didn't know you were into sports, Sterling."

"I'm not," Sterling huffed. "I had a meeting in the

area and with what I want to discuss with you, it's important that we have some privacy."

Isaac met his eyes. "Well, if it's anything like what we discussed yesterday, perhaps I should start drinking now."

He lifted his hand to call over a waiter.

But when the man arrived, Sterling beat him to the punch.

"We'll have two club sodas with lime and two chicken Caesar salads."

"Good thing I like salad," Isaac muttered as the waiter walked away. "So if you won't let me drink or order my own food, why don't you tell me why we're here?"

Sterling loosened his tie and looked uncomfortable. He cleared his throat. "For an apology."

A sudden roar of laughter erupted from the next table over.

"Excuse me," Isaac said. "I don't think I heard correctly."

Sterling cleared his throat again and leaned against the table. "I'm here for an apology." He held up a hand. "Not yours, mine."

"I don't understand," Isaac replied.

"The document that Autumn found is a fake."

"That's what I was trying to tell you yesterday," Isaac retorted in an exasperated tone.

"But what you don't know is that I planted it."

"You did? Why?"

"I was trying to help my daughter. I knew it was her

that was running an internal smear campaign against you."

"I'm not surprised," Isaac said. "She was constantly trying to throw me under the bus."

"Even worse, a few weeks ago she gave me some trumped-up documents, similar to the one that Autumn found, to prove you were guilty of securities fraud," Sterling continued. "I knew when I hired you ten years ago that you were above reproach, and I still believe that so I brought Autumn on board to prove us both right, and in the meantime, I hoped that Felicia would realize what she'd done."

Isaac sat back in his chair, incredulous at what he was hearing. "So you try to help Felicia by ruining me? That doesn't make any sense, Sterling."

"I know," he admitted. "But I had hoped that she would confess to everything yesterday. That's why I invited her to the meeting. When she didn't, I had to go through with the charade of dismissal."

"Charade?" Isaac swallowed hard. "Does that mean I have my old job back?"

Sterling nodded. "If you'll accept my apology, that is."

Isaac knit his brows. "There's always a catch with you, isn't there?"

Sterling chuckled and waited to speak until the waiter had set down their beverages.

"Then let me sweeten the deal. There's a little thing called a partnership at the end of this rainbow. Does that make accepting my humble apology more palatable?"

Isaac stirred the ice cubes in his glass of club soda

with a straw, buying time. Sterling's offer seemed genuine, but with everything the man had just told him, he still wasn't sure.

"Do you think I'm ready for the responsibility of a partner?"

Sterling nodded. "You've been ready for months, Isaac. You're the best investment analyst on staff. You've got the keenest eye for the moneymaker stocks and clients love you. What more could I ask for?"

"Oh, I don't know. Maybe a son-in-law for Felicia," Isaac replied with a shrug.

Sterling nearly choked. "What?"

"Your daughter has the hots for me, and I'm not interested. If I come back, I need you to tell her to lay off."

"That won't be necessary," he assured, sounding relieved. "I fired her this morning."

Isaac tipped his chair back, almost hitting someone at the opposite table. "You fired your own daughter, why?"

"Because somewhere along the way, I failed her, which was likely the reason she tried to destroy you. If I don't get her some help now, I could be next."

Isaac blew out a breath. Being offered a partnership at Paxton, the firm he'd given so much of his time and talents to, was a dream come true. All his sacrifices would pay off. But he had some confessing to do of his own.

"You know, a part of me almost understands why you felt you had to give Felicia every chance to make things right because I'm a dad, too. I adopted two teenagers about six months ago. Their names are Devon and Deshauna."

Isaac paused a beat and waited for Sterling's reaction.

"I know."

Isaac folded his arms. "How?"

"I make it a point to know everything about my employees, even some things they are trying to hide. That's why I knew you couldn't be deceitful. Anybody that could give up his freedom to become a father to two teenagers is a man I know I can trust."

"It was kind of scary at first, being a dad. And I'll still make a ton of mistakes. But I love them and they love me."

"Now you need to take the same leap with Autumn."

"You know about her, too, huh?"

Sterling nodded. "You think she let you down, but in all truth, she didn't. I urge you not to let pride get in the way of love. I did and for twenty-five years I've regretted it."

"Ms. Witterman?"

"Isn't she a beauty?"

Isaac laughed. "I wish you both the best of luck."

Sterling pushed back his chair and stood. "You can have your second chance, too, Isaac. The best way to win a woman's heart is to be the man she's always been waiting for. Just don't wait twenty-five years to do it."

"Any idea where I can find her?"

"She mentioned she would be moving on to her next assignment in a few days. That's all I know," he replied, shrugging into his coat.

The waiter approached with the salads they had ordered earlier.

"Wait. What about your food?"

Sterling pushed his chair back against the table and wrapped a plaid scarf around his neck.

"I'm having lunch with Eleanor. Take mine to go and share it with your kids." He started to walk away, but turned back to Isaac. "See you at 8:00 a.m. sharp tomorrow?"

Isaac smiled gratefully. "I'll be there and thanks for everything."

As soon as Sterling was gone, Isaac instructed the waiter to package up both salads. With a very busy afternoon ahead, there was no time to spare. He needed to track down Autumn before he lost her for good.

Autumn kicked her sneakered toe against the front of her suitcase. Her flight to Seattle had been delayed for a few hours and rather than suffer at the airport, she had decided to wait it out at her apartment. The doorman was in the process of getting her a car service to JFK and would call her with the details.

The travel delay was annoying for sure, but she was also grateful for it for no other reason than she hoped she would hear from Isaac again. She stared at the phone again, willing it to ring, and wanting to kick herself for not answering his calls and texts yesterday. Now the phone was silent, mocking her cowardice.

Sterling had kept his end of the bargain. He didn't let on who had found the report that got him suspended.

Now she had to uphold her part of the deal and get out of town, so she could bury her fears in her next case.

Autumn jumped at the sound of a knock on her door. "This is it," she muttered softly under her breath, stretching her arms against fatigue as she left the couch.

"What time is the car coming? The flight leaves in ninety minutes," she called out as she opened the door.

When she saw who was on the other side, she took a step back over the threshold.

"You're not going anywhere until we talk."

"Isaac! How did you know I was still here?"

"You're not the only one who can pay off the doorman." His lips curved into a smile, his eyes twinkling. "He's expensive, but very effective, don't you agree?"

Autumn felt her face burn, but she refused to acknowledge his comment. She dropped her hand from the knob and stepped aside so Isaac could enter the room.

When the door was closed, she leaned against it, glad for the support. He was wearing that cologne again. The same one he wore on the night they made love for the first time.

"I'm sorry about your suspension."

"You should be. You're the one who caused it."

Autumn's eyes dipped low and the blood rushed to her face. She started to open her mouth to explain, but Isaac held up his hand to stop her.

"Let me guess. You were only doing your job, right?"

She nodded, but then tilted her head. "Why don't you sound mad?"

He laughed. "Because we both got played…and it's wonderful!"

She shouldered off the door and stood before him. "What are you talking about, Isaac?"

His eyes bored into hers and there was a hint of seriousness in them. "Did I ever tell you how cute you look when you get confused?"

"You're a stockbroker, not a lawyer, so don't change the subject," Autumn warned.

"Felicia told me you're a private investigator."

Autumn cringed inwardly. "And I suppose you believed her?"

"At first, I didn't want to. I kept calling and calling to try to talk with you but you never answered."

"I'm sorry. I didn't know what to say. I didn't want to lie anymore and I couldn't tell you the truth under the terms of the contract I had with Sterling."

"I understand."

"You do? Well, how did we both get played then?"

"Sterling used both of us to try to convince Felicia to stop harassing me. He knew the document was fake because he planted it in the files himself!"

Autumn shook her head and then she started to laugh. "I can't believe it."

"Neither could I at first. Felicia had originally given Sterling some reports meant to incriminate me, but he was suspicious that she'd doctored them up somehow. So he hired you in the hopes that at any point during the investigation she would confess to what she'd tried to do. Yesterday was her last chance."

"Where is Felicia now?"

"On the unemployment line, I suppose. Sterling fired her sometime between yesterday and today."

"And what about you?"

"That's the best news of all. You're looking at the first African-American partner at Paxton Investment Securities!"

Autumn clasped her hands around his neck. "Isaac, that's terrific! Congratulations."

"You know what would be even better?"

She laid her head upon his chest and listened to his heartbeat.

"Coming home to you every evening and making love to you far into the night."

Autumn looked into his eyes. "I would love that, too, but I've accepted another assignment."

He clasped her hands in his. "Do you have to leave so soon?"

She stepped back, praying that her next words wouldn't hurt him. "But I love my career, Isaac. There's more crooks to catch and hopefully this time, they're real."

"I'm not asking you to give up anything." He dove into one of his pockets. "Just take this."

When Isaac opened his hand, there was a key in his palm. "You'll always have a home with us. When you come back, I'll be here. Waiting to show you how much I love you."

Tears sprang to Autumn's eyes and she had to fight to hold them back. "I love you, too." She took the key and held it tightly as she clung to him.

"Can I tell you another secret? Autumn isn't even my real name."

He smiled and stroked her hair. "Then what is it, my super sexy spy?"

"I'll tell you, but it's a crime if you kiss me for the answer," she teased.

Isaac's lips found hers. "Guilty as charged."

* * * * *